AGAINST THE

AMULET BOOKS · NEW YORK

AMY IGNATOW

ODDS

ABRAMS The Art of Books
115 West 18th Street, New York, NY 10011
abramsbooks.com

To Kit, Nate, Jennifer, Sarah, Colleen, Nicole, and Sue
for providing decades of odd inspiration

The Muelle

Local Muellersville Educator Wanted for Arson

The Muellersville Police Department is seeking the whereabouts of local substitute teacher Ryan Friend, 28, who is wanted for questioning in regard to a series of arsons. He was last witnessed fleeing the scene of a house fire on Tall Oaks Drive.

The homeowner, Angela Gross, was able to escape the blaze but suffered from smoke inhalation. "I have no idea why anyone would want to do this to us," the single mother said from her hospital bed. "But I hope they catch the guy before he can hurt anyone else."

"He seemed like a nice enough man," said Charlene Beckerman, who went on three dates with Mr. Friend two years ago but chose not to continue the relationship because "he took his yo-yo everywhere and that was kind of weird."

His students were less charitable. "One time he sent me to the assistant principal's office and I hardly did anything," said Izaak Marcus, an eighth grader at Deborah Read Middle School who often had Mr. Friend as a substitute teacher. "And you could tell that even though he was saying, 'Izaak, go see Mr. Deutsch,' what he really meant was, 'Izaak, I totally want to set you on fire!'"

Local police did not want to speculate about the motive behind Mr. Friend's alleged arsonist tendencies. "Look, we just want to ask the guy some questions," Chief Gary Romaine told *The Muellersville Sun*, "while maybe holding on to a fire extinguisher."

THE DAILY WHUT?

WHERE IS RYAN FRIEND?

That's right, faithful readers, The Hammer has made the artistic choice to press down on the CAPS LOCK button because I can't believe that a suspected arsonist is still running around Muellersville. Where will he strike next? Whose house or car will go up in flames? Why aren't the police more concerned? WHERE'S THE MANHUNT?

I'll tell you why there isn't a manhunt. It's because RYAN FRIEND IS INNOCENT. Isn't it just so convenient that the only suspect that the police have is a substitute teacher with no friends or family nearby. The only person that *The Muellersville Sun* could find to say anything about him was some lady who went on three dates with him two years ago. But longtime readers of *The Daily Whut* know very well that *The Muellersville Sun* is in the pocket of local law enforcement and possesses the journalistic integrity of a ham sandwich. A HAM SANDWICH WITH NO JOURNALISTIC INTEGRITY.

Oh, Hammer, you say, you're making crazy, unfounded statements again. Am I? AM I REALLY? Let's all remember the time that I was right about Freshtush toilet paper rolls getting shorter so that the company could make more money per roll. My track record is spotless, which is more than I can say for The Muellersville Ham Sandwich.

Ryan Friend never once showed any violent tendencies. He was a substitute teacher who loved yo-yos and occasionally sent a deserving little twerp to the principal's office. He wasn't some highly trained firebug with the ability to vanish into thin air.

WHERE IS RYAN FRIEND?

Ever questioning,
The Hammer

_____

OKAY, LET'S GO OVER IT AGAIN." JAY WAS PACING the length of his room, unable to contain his energy. Nick hadn't seen his best friend this worked up since The Hammer's blog had convinced him that there was methylphenidate in the Muellersville town water supply. That time Jay had worked himself into such a frenzy that he'd begun to hyperventilate. Nick's mom had made Jay breathe into a paper bag to calm down. Nick scanned Jay's room for a paper bag.

"I don't know what else to tell you," he said. It was too early in the morning for Jay's energy.

"Nick. Nick. NICK. Last night you saw AN INVISIBLE MAN," Jay yelled, throwing his hands up in the air. Nick thought about telling him to quiet down, but it wasn't as if Jay's parents weren't used to their son's nonsensical rants. They were probably tuning him out, as usual.

"Well, technically I didn't actually see anything," Nick pointed out.

"Amazing. AMAZING. And not true—you say that he picked up Mr. Friend, so you saw Mr. Friend LEVITATING. Now tell me that wasn't amazing!"

Nick had to grin. "Okay, that was pretty cool."

"Pretty cool?" Jay threw his hands up in the air. "Nick, old sport, your gift for understatement is magnificent. So let's review. You, Martina, Farshad, *and* the Amish lad, *and* the bus driver, *and* the ravishing Miss Daniesha Parker all have superpowers."

"Jay, you seriously have to stop calling Cookie 'ravishing.' I'm pretty sure she doesn't like it."

"Nonsense, all women love to be complimented. Especially ravishing ones with superpowers."

Nick sighed. "I wouldn't call them superpowers, exactly. They're not that super." Nick thought a moment. "Except the horse. I think Abe's horse had super speed."

"I . . . I can't even deal with that right now. But Amish Abe can *control animals and protect them from a flaming inferno*??? And the bus driver is INVISIBLE."

"Yeah, but he can't seem to get visible again. That's not so super."

"Wait." Jay froze. "Wait wait wait. Was the bus driver naked?"

"What? Ew! No. I don't think so. How would I know? I couldn't see him."

"Ugh, Nicholas, you are too squeamish about nudity. It's the body's natural state. If I had my druthers, I'd be naked all the time." Jay spread his spindly arms and gazed off into the distance, as if he were imagining a world where he could be unencumbered by clothing. Then he looked perplexed. "Although I don't know what I'd do for pockets."

"Maybe a purse? Like, a manly one?" Nick asked. Sometimes he wondered how Jay roped him into these conversations, but it was usually pretty entertaining to go with the flow.

"That would give me a strange tan line."

"I don't recall ever seeing you tan."

"It would give me an odd burn line. So what you're saying, though, is that the bus driver could have been naked."

"I don't know." Nick thought a moment. "Martina would probably have told us if he was naked, right?" Martina was the only one who had been able to see the invisible bus driver. Maybe the power to change her eye color had something to do with her ability to see Ed?

"Hmmm. The alluring Miss Martina seems like the sort who would be good at keeping secrets about nudity." Jay flopped down on top of the bed, and then flopped around some more to get comfortable. He looked like a fish that had just been pulled out of the water and placed on a dry dock. "Let's say the driver isn't naked," Jay mused.

"Yes, let's say that," Nick agreed.

"If he isn't, that means that it is within his power to turn other things invisible." Jay jumped back to his feet. "Just like it's within your power to move things with you, like your clothing and small pebbles that you are holding, when you teleport!!!"

"Shhh!" Nick said, his eyes darting to Jay's bedroom door.

Jay scoffed. "Please, it's as if you haven't been here a million times. They're not listening in." He raised his voice. "AND THAT'S WHEN WE WILL ALL SUBMIT TO OUR ALIEN OVERLORDS. WE WILL GIVE THEM ALL THE CORN CHOWDER AND THEY SHALL REWARD US WITH THE EURASIAN STEPPE." Jay fell silent and looked at Nick. "I could tell them to their faces about your power and they still wouldn't hear me."

He had a point. For as long as Nick had known Jay (forever), the Carpenters had never paid too much attention to him, as long as he got good grades and tested well. Still, Jay needed to get in the habit of being a little more discreet. If Cookie Parker heard him talking in public about their powers, she'd end the little weirdo.

Nick grabbed Jay's wrist and looked at the watch he always wore. "Molly is going to be here soon," he said. "She's probably already on her way." He didn't want to keep his aunt waiting and felt bad enough about leaving his mother alone in her hospital room the night before.

"How long are you staying with your aunts?" Jay asked. "You know you could just stay here until your house is ready. My parents wouldn't care."

"Thanks," Nick said, "but my mom is going to stay with them, and I want to be with her." The doctor at the hospital had assured Nick and his aunts that his mom was going to be fine, but he was still worried about her. She'd looked so fragile. Plus his aunts always made good food like spaghetti and meatballs, while the Carpenters had once pressured Nick into eating raw sea urchin. Avoiding that was alone worth sleeping on the nursery futon at Molly and Jilly's house.

"I understand, old boy," Jay said, "but you have to promise to tell me the minute there are any developments on your . . . odd situation."

Nick promised and headed out to wait on the curb for his aunt. As soon as he sat down, he felt the four-inch shift to the left as he inadvertently teleported.

"Oh, come on," he muttered under his breath, gripping the curb with both of his hands in a desperate attempt to stay put before teleporting four inches to the left again. "You have got to be kidding me."

FARSHAD RAJAVI STARED IN DISMAY AT THE RUINS OF what just one minute before had been his father's functioning laptop. The space bar was crushed, and the practice test on the screen flickered and blurred. Farshad stared for a moment at his hands before closing his eyes.

I'll just tell him I dropped something on it, he decided, and grimaced at the thought of lying to either of his parents. Lying was something that Farshad had never done before the bus accident had turned him into a great big freak. Sure, there had been plenty of times when he hadn't been completely honest, but flat-out lying was new.

He opened his eyes and looked around the room for something that would be heavy enough to cause the damage that his abnormally strong thumbs had caused. There were a few heavy-looking books, a framed photo of Farshad with his family in front of the Azadi Tower in Tehran, and a trophy from when he used to play soccer. He picked up the trophy. Plastic. Too light. The books weren't going to cut it either. He was going to have to take the framed photograph and let it drop to the floor. *The glass will probably smash*, Farshad thought, *and then maybe they'll be so upset that the photo is messed up that they won't even think too hard about the laptop.*

Farshad took the frame off the wall and looked at the

smiling faces in the photo, which had been taken while they were visiting family a few years ago. He placed the frame back on the hook on the wall, taking care not to put too much pressure on it with his thumbs. What had he been thinking? And why had he never considered taking up bowling as a sport? Having a bowling ball would have been really useful right about now. Farshad sighed, shut the laptop, and headed downstairs. He'd just use the computer lab at school to finish the test and figure out what to do about the laptop later.

"You're up early." His mother looked at him worriedly as he grabbed his jacket. "What is up?"

"I'm just going to school a little early," Farshad told her. "There's a pre-homeroom study group meetup." *Lying lies told by a lying liar.*

"Ah, yes," Dr. Rajavi nodded. "The exam is coming up. Are you ready?"

"I will be," he said, grabbing a croissant from the bag on top of the fridge and shoving it into his mouth. If there was one thing his parents would never stop him from doing, it was studying. He gave his mom a quick kiss on the cheek and headed out the front door.

Farshad kept his head down as he walked to school, just like he'd done since the fourth grade, when he'd become the class pariah because his parents were Persian (or "terrorists" as his idiot classmates liked to whisper behind his back . . . and say out loud in front of his face). Stooping down made Farshad appear to be shorter than he was so that people would notice him less, which, when he thought about it, was another type of lying. But lying to protect yourself seemed a lot better than telling the truth and getting hurt. Look at Mr. Friend. If he had just been able to control his power and then lie about being able to set things on fire with his mind, he wouldn't be . . .

Where was he? Where had they taken Mr. Friend? And who were *they*?

The ride home from the farm had been pretty quiet. Nick Gross had been worried about his mom, Cookie Parker had been cursing under her breath as she picked bits of straw out of her curls, and Martina Saltis had never been much of a talker in the first place. She had just looked out the window as the farmland turned into the suburbs, her eyes changing from blue to green to brown to a very disconcerting shade of violet. Farshad had a thousand questions and not much faith that any of his newfound Comrades in Lame Powers would be able to answer them, so he stayed quiet as well.

Abe had dropped them off near the school so they could all walk home. At the time, Farshad had been relieved to get out of the buggy (that horse was *fast*) and glad to have the short walk home to think about everything that had happened before he sneaked back into his house. When he got there, his parents hadn't even realized that he was missing. They had just assumed he'd been in his room, studying. It made sense; besides running, studying in his room was all Farshad did, really. He thought about Cookie Parker and how she was always surrounded by a crowd of friends. She probably hadn't been able to sneak back home so easily.

Good, Farshad thought. They'd been through too much together for him to hate her like he used to, but the thought of Cookie getting into trouble still made him smile.

Farshad passed by a janitor and some teachers prepping lessons in their rooms. He was eager to finish the practice test; he might not be able to control the unbelievable strength in his thumbs, but he could do well on the exam, and right now it felt good to be in control of something in his life.

"No, Officer, I haven't seen Ryan since the accident." Farshad heard Mrs. Whitaker's voice. He stopped walking. "I just assumed he was recuperating. You don't really believe that he had anything to do with those fires, do you?"

Farshad pretended to open a locker near Mrs. Whitaker's classroom door and peeked in. She was talking with a uniformed police officer.

"We're just gathering information, ma'am." The officer said. "Had Mr. Friend been acting strangely before the accident?"

"No! I don't think so. I didn't know him that well. He was just a substitute."

"I understand. Did he ever mention any friends? Hobbies? Places he liked to go to when he wasn't at work?"

"Tahiti? Ha-ha, no, kidding, that's where I would like to go when I'm not at work."

"I hear that, ha-ha. Well, if you can think of anywhere he'd be or any person he'd spend time with . . ."

"Actually"—Mrs. Whitaker thought a moment—"I think he might have been seeing Maggie Zelle. You know. Romantically. Although I doubt it was anything serious."

"We've already spoken to Ms. Zelle," the officer said, "and she knows about as much as we do."

"Oh no, she knows way more—she's a science teacher, ha-ha-ha!"

"Ha-ha! Well, here's my card, let me know."

"Will do, Officer," Mrs. Whitaker said. Farshad heard the policeman heading toward the door and stared intently at the combination lock in front of him. The officer gave him a suspicious glance before heading down the hall. Farshad walked quickly to the computer lab. He logged into the practice test site and tried and failed to concentrate. He looked at his thumbs.

Where was Mr. Friend? And what was happening to him?

EXCUSE ME?" COOKIE PARKER GAVE EMMA LEE A hard stare. Sure, Cookie had been eating ice cream last night with a social pariah and a complete nobody, but did Emma have proof? Was there a photo? A video? Other witnesses to corroborate her story? Because if not, Cookie was pretty sure it didn't happen. Even though it did.

"I . . . I asked how you liked your ice cream," Emma said, giving Cookie her own version of a hard stare. *Amateur.*

"I like it cold," Cookie said, talking to Emma as if she were a small, annoying child. "How do you like your ice cream?"

"I meant . . ." Emma looked at Addison and Claire, who had stopped primping in front of their locker mirrors and were instead watching the conversation with growing curiosity. "I meant I thought I saw you yesterday," Emma said, weakening. "Eating ice cream . . . with people."

"Is that where you were?" Claire asked. "Did you go out for ice cream without us?"

"Yes," Cookie said, rolling her eyes. "I totally took advantage of a school evacuation to make a bunch of new friends and eat ice cream with them." Addison and Claire giggled. Emma looked confused.

"But I saw you . . ." she started.

"Did you say hi?" Cookie asked.

"No, I was with my family . . ."

"So, what, your family doesn't like me, so you can't say hi to me and my awesome new friends?"

"No . . . no, it wasn't like that . . ."

"Okay, so what was it like? Did you see a black person and just assume it was me? I get that. We really all do look alike." Cookie was getting angry, as if Emma had really seen some random other black person and mistaken them for her.

"Oh no. No no no no," Emma said, backing up. "I was probably wrong. It wasn't you."

"Whatever," Cookie said, and spotted Martina about twenty feet behind Emma. Martina waved. Cookie turned away without waving back.

"It totally wasn't you," Emma repeated.

"This is boring," Cookie said, turning to leave. "I'm going to the bathroom." Claire and Addison quickly walked away with her. Sometimes Cookie wondered if they would remember to go to the bathroom if it weren't for her. One day they were going to have to thank her for keeping their kidneys from bursting.

"That was weird," Addison commented.

"Sometimes Emma can be such a little freak," Claire scoffed.

"Where were you yesterday anyway?" Addison asked.

Cookie was ready. Keep it simple. "Ugh, I lost my phone when we were running out of the school yesterday and then my mom wouldn't let me leave the house to look for it. Some kid found it and called my mom on it last night." Cookie knew that there was a pretty good chance that Nick or one of the others (*probably Jay Carpenter, please not Jay Carpenter*) would try to talk to her at school. If Addison or Claire saw them then she could just say it was about returning her phone.

You had to think of these things ahead of time—the last thing Cookie needed was to be caught unawares. She'd dealt with enough of that recently, thank you very much.

For a moment Cookie considered feeling bad about making Emma Lee out to be some sort of racist crazy person, but really, the fact was that the only reason Emma had mentioned seeing Cookie with Martina and Farshad was to embarrass her in front of her friends. And that wasn't nice. And in Cookie's book it was okay to be not nice to not-nice people who were out to get her.

Addison and Claire started debating about inviting Emma to their upcoming study group, even though she was acting weird. She always took copious notes and performed really well on exams, and they'd already asked her to join them . . . they chattered on and Cookie felt drained. She'd only slept a few hours the night before, unable to stop her brain from recalling everything that had happened on Abe Zook's farm. The terrifying ride in the horse-drawn buggy. The invisible bus driver that only Martina could see. Mr. Friend, looking completely unhinged. Ms. Zelle, the fight, the fire, the barnyard animals calmly following Abe through the fire to safety. JUMPING OUT OF THE SECOND FLOOR OF A BURNING BARN. Hearing everyone's stupid thoughts.

Cookie splashed some water on her face and leaned her forehead against the bathroom mirror. It took her a moment to realize that Addison and Claire had stopped talking.

"Hey, Cooks, are you okay?" Addison asked gingerly.

Not even close to being okay, Cookie thought. "Yeah," she said, "my head still hurts a little."

"Oh!" Addison and Claire said together, and immediately giggled over having the exact same reaction. "Well, your hair is still super cute," Addison said.

"Thank goodness for that," Cookie said, smiling. Claire linked her arm with Cookie's. "Let's go to class," she said.

Exit the bathroom. Make a left away from the classroom. Head down the hall. Make a right and go into the stairwell. Go under the steps.

Cookie heard Martina's voice as if she were whispering directly into her ear. It was overwhelming, and she had to clench her teeth to keep from screaming at Martina (wherever she was) to get out of her head, because there was no way that the freaky-eyed girl wasn't deliberately sending her a message.

Exit the bathroom. Make a left away from the classroom. Head down the hall . . .

"I think I'm going to hit up the nurse for an aspirin or something," Cookie said, slipping her arm out of Claire's.

"Do you want us to go with you?" Addison asked with a concerned look.

"I don't know," Cookie said. "Aspirin are pretty heavy, but I think I might be able to handle it. How about I text you if it's too much for me." She rolled her eyes dramatically and Addison and Claire laughed and headed to class.

Cookie turned left away from their classroom and headed down the hall until she made a right to get to the stairwell. Underneath stood Martina, looking very pleased with herself.

"You heard me!" Martina said, her blue eyes shining. "That's extraordinary."

"Yes, I heard you," Cookie hissed angrily. "Now NEVER. DO. THAT. AGAIN." She rubbed her temples and slumped against the wall of the Understeps. "You don't know how disturbing it is to have someone else's voice in your head."

"I apologize, I asked her to do it," a male voice said.

Cookie froze. "Martina," she whispered, panicked, grabbing the girl's arm, "I'm hearing someone else and they're not thinking about directions! It's like they're talking right to me."

"Oh, that's Ed," Martina said, patting Cookie's hand awkwardly. "Sorry, I should have told you that he was standing next to you."

"Sorry," Invisible Ed said.

"I hate you both so much, you have no idea," Cookie growled, letting Martina go.

"I'm really very sorry," Ed said again. He sounded like he was a few feet away. "But I need to speak to you. To all of you. We need to discuss our . . . situation. Will you help to get the others together?"

"Sure," Cookie said, taking her phone out of her pocket. "I will use this handy modern communication device to contact them without having to invade anyone's personal private brainspace." She pressed the icon to access her email account.

"No!" Ed put his invisible hand on Cookie's and she instinctively jerked away, immediately befuddled by her inability to shoot an angry look at him because she didn't quite know where he was.

"I'm sorry, but we can't use modern communication devices to discuss these things," Ed explained. "They could be monitoring our accounts."

"They?" Cookie asked. "Who are they? You sound like a crazy person."

Ed sighed. "Being invisible is crazy. Being able to read minds is *crazy*. Whatever she can do"—Cookie looked over to where Martina was happily scribbling in her sketchbook—"is crazy. And yet here we are. Please trust me just long enough to get everyone together so we can talk this out and I'll tell you everything I know."

"How do I know you're not just getting us together to put us in a lab or something and do experiments because we're all great big freaks now?" Cookie crossed her arms and glared in the general direction of Ed's voice.

"Actually, that's what I want to do." Ed said matter-of-factly.

"Oh." Cookie was at a loss.

"I'll get Nick and Farshad!" Jay Carpenter popped his head out from the stairway above them.

"GAAAH!" Cookie yelped and heard Ed gasp "What the—" under his breath before falling silent.

Even Martina looked slightly disturbed by Jay's sudden appearance. "How long have you been listening in?" she asked Jay, who scrambled down the remaining stairs to join them.

"Long enough to know that you're both talking to an invisible bus driver." Jay bowed toward a wall. "Hello, good see-through sir, I am Jay Carpenter and it is an honor to make your acquaintance." He held out his hand to shake and got nothing. Cookie rubbed her temples.

"Oh, Daniesha," Jay started, "I do apologize for giving you a fright, but . . ."

"Shut. It." Cookie said without looking up.

"How many people know about this?" Ed asked from her right side. He sounded very nervous.

"Just us and Jay," Cookie said, at a loss to explain exactly why this little freak show knew so much about their situation.

"And have no fear, my dear transparent new friend, I am the soul of discretion," Jay said, finally putting down his unshaken hand. "I will adjourn to the classrooms and gather our compatriots. And I will do so with subtlety and stealth!" The little freak show dashed off.

"Can he be trusted?" Ed asked.

"Yes," Martina said at the same time that Cookie said, "Not as far as I can throw him." Cookie shot a look to Martina, who smiled back and continued drawing in her book.

"This is going to be another weird day, isn't it?" Cookie asked to no one in particular.

"Oh yes," Martina said never raising her eyes from her drawing. "I'd say we're in for a lot more of those."

It was a container of liquid. When Gabe saw it he got very scared and said I'd brought too much.

Ed, you've got to get this back to Auxano before they realize it's missing.

And the container spilled when we got into the bus accident?

NICK WAS A LITTLE SURPRISED AT HOW FAST COOKIE agreed to go to Philadelphia to meet up with some random scientist that an invisible guy had recommended. Martina was up for the trip, although in the short time he had known Martina she seemed amenable to pretty much everything. Nothing seemed to rattle her. Jay, of course, was chomping at the bit to go to the lab in Philadelphia, although no one had really invited him.

Farshad had remained mostly silent throughout Ed's proposal, occasionally glancing down at his hands. Nick wondered what he was thinking.

"I can drive you to Philadelphia on Saturday," Ed promised. "We'll go, we'll talk to my brother, and be back in just a few hours. I really think he can give us some answers and help us to get through this."

"I can't just up and go to Philadelphia," Nick said. "My mom is getting out of the hospital, and my house is full of smoke damage. My family needs me and they are going to notice if I just disappear for a day."

"Oh please," Cookie said with a dismissive wave of her arm, "just tell them that you need to go to a study group or that you're hanging out with this little freak." She gestured to Jay, who blew her a kiss.

"They need me. My mom needs me right now." Nick was

getting angry. He felt himself inadvertently teleport four inches to his left.

"It's all right, old boy, it's all right." Jay said, resting his hand on Nick's arm. "Does he really need to be there?"

"I'd like to get all of you there," Ed said as the second-period bell rang.

"We should go to class," Farshad said, ducking his head to get out of the Understeps.

"Will you be able to come to Philadelphia?" Ed asked.

"We're going to be late," Farshad said, heading down the hallway. Nick shook Jay off his arm and followed Farshad. They turned down a hall and were alone.

"So—are you going?" Nick had to work to keep up with Farshad. The guy had long legs.

"I don't think so," Farshad said. "The exam is next week and I need to study."

"Really?" Nick stopped walking. "That's your reason?"

"What, am I supposed to fail out of school?" Farshad asked.

"No?" Nick asked, suddenly finding himself four inches to his left. It happened as fast as a blink. Farshad reached out to grab Nick's arm. Nick was grateful for the anchor. If someone was holding on to him he wouldn't disappear, that much had been made terribly clear when he'd tried to teleport his mother out of their burning house. Farshad steered Nick into an empty classroom.

"Look," he said, "I just don't know if we can trust the bus driver."

"Ed."

"Whatever. He's the one who was using a school bus full of kids to transport what turned out to be highly dangerous chemicals. He's the one who was keeping a guy who can light fires with his mind in a highly flammable barn. Ed has not shown himself to be a guy with particularly good judgment."

"So what are we supposed to do?" Nick asked, trying not to sound like a panicky whiner.

Farshad looked at his hands. "I don't know. Nothing. The last time we tried to 'do something' we ended up in the middle of Amish country in a burning barn. We're lucky to be alive. Let's just learn how to control our . . . abilities, keep our heads down, and act like all this never happened."

Nick liked the idea. Go home, help his aunts to clean up his house, take care of his mom while she recovered. Pretend he'd never been in an accident. Maybe after a while it would all just turn into a story he'd tell nonchalantly, *Oh yeah, I was in a bus accident once time, but I was fine, it was no big deal. I didn't develop the freakish ability to teleport myself four inches to the left or potentially much farther if I'm feeling stressed . . .*

But would it really work? "I don't know, man," he said. "I don't think this is the sort of thing we can just ignore."

"Okay," Farshad said, "then I'll just spend all my time thinking about that time we nearly died and coming up with new and exciting ways to put myself in harm's way by doing dangerous and stupid things. That seems like a good use of my time."

"I mean, we'd just be going to Philadelphia . . ."

The bell rang again. They were late for class. "Would you rather just fail out of school?" Farshad asked, his voice rising. "There are very few things in this world that we can control and how we do academically is one of them. I'm going to class." He left the room.

Nick sat for another minute. He'd been in a bus accident, and his house had caught on fire. His English teacher would probably be okay with him being a little late, and he had to calm down before he left the room so that he wouldn't accidentally teleport himself into a locker on his way to class.

COOKIE HAD AGREED TO GO TO PHILADELPHIA, NOT because, as Jay said, they needed her "street smarts." "Oh," she said, "so you think because I'm black that I naturally have street smarts?"

"Oh no," Jay said, "Oh no no no no no, I just mean that you know which streets to take because you moved here from Philadelphia."

Of course. She was always going to be the girl from Philly, even though she had moved to Muellersville when she was five. The truth was that she couldn't navigate her way across Philadelphia without looking at her phone (something that had been made painfully clear by her inability to find the jewelry store while she and Claire were playing hooky during the class field trip). But she had always liked being thought of as a Philly girl, a city kid who was smarter and quicker and savvier than the dumb-dumb country mice of Muellersville. It was the reason people liked her. She knew things they didn't know, like where to find the coolest jewelry in Philadelphia.

"She's going to come with us because she doesn't want to hear people thinking about directions anymore," Martina said without looking up from her book. She didn't talk much, but Cookie was beginning to notice that when she did talk, whatever she said was extremely accurate. She was almost the complete opposite of Claire and Addison.

"Piffle," Jay said. "Why on earth would someone not want powers? That's ridiculous, you all just need a little help in harnessing them. But have no fear, I am here to help . . ."

The bell rang. "We'd better go," Cookie said and turned to Jay. "Try to get Nick to come."

Cookie headed to the science lab, which was the last class that she wanted to be late to. Everyone was seated and Ms. Zelle gave Cookie a quizzical look as she slipped into the classroom.

"Sorry," Cookie muttered.

"Your friends said that you weren't feeling well," Ms. Zelle said.

"I'm okay now," Cookie said. *Be cool, girl. Act like you haven't seen her going all martial arts on an invisible man. Everything is normal. Just go to your seat.*

Emma Lee was in her seat. HER seat. Cookie always sat between Addison and Claire. Cookie could feel everyone in the class watching her. She held her head up high and headed for the only other empty seat in the room, which was in the back with the Farm Kids. Paul Yoder eyed her suspiciously as she sat down next to him. This was so humiliating. She was going to have to deal with Emma later.

Claire turned around and mouthed *Sorry!* to Cookie. But apparently not sorry enough to save her a seat. Cookie fumed as Ms. Zelle began to speak.

"Okay everybody, we all know what's happening next week!"

"The exam," the class droned in unison. Izaak Marcus rolled his eyes and pretended to fall asleep.

"Don't sound too excited. So we all know that they are the national exams, and not the statewide exams, right? Can anyone tell me the difference?"

Cookie took out her notebook and pretended to take notes on whatever Ms. Zelle was saying. She could feel the weight of her cell phone in her pocket and itched to take it out so she could compose a thoughtful text to Addison and Claire on the importance of loyalty in a friendship and how apparently they were loyal to Emma Lee now, and have fun with that, maybe she'd make friends with a damp gym towel and have exactly the same experience . . . of course Cookie would never actually send a text like that. No, she was just going to ignore them until they were bending over backward to be nice to her.

Years ago Cookie and her mom had been in Philadelphia visiting with her cousins. Zakiya and Nadijah had been dancing to some music, and when Cookie didn't recognize the song, they'd made fun of her. "I guess they don't have black people music in Amish country," Nadijah had said.

"Do you just listen to country music?" Zakiya laughed.

"Do you know how to square dance?" Nadijah said, and they had practically fallen over laughing at their jokes.

Cookie had burst into tears and run to find her mother, which just made her older cousins laugh more.

"Oh, Cookie," her mom had said after she'd calmed down. "Never let anyone see that they've upset you. If people know that they've hurt your feelings, that gives them power over you."

So of course Cookie wasn't going to let Addison and Claire know that they'd pretty much stabbed her with a million little knives while she was already down! RECOVERING FROM A MAJOR ACCIDENT.

Cookie felt eyes on her. Sam Stoltzfus was staring at her. She glared back at him.

"Ooo, ooo," he said under his breath, making the monkey noise while bending his elbow to scratch his own armpit and contorting his face. "Ooo."

Izaak turned around and looked at Cookie. "Is that inbred messing with you?"

"Mind your business, jungle fever," Sam growled at him.

"Mr. Stoltzfus, Mr. Marcus, is this something that's pertinent to next week's exam?" Ms. Zelle asked from the front of the class. Izaak sat up straight and smiled as though he hadn't said anything. Sam glowered. Ms. Zelle gave them a stern look and continued writing on the board.

Cookie looked back down at her notebook. Never let them see that they've upset you.

NICK MANAGED TO AVOID EVERYONE FOR THE REST of the day. (Except Jay. It was impossible to avoid Jay.) After his last class he gathered up his things and walked to the shortcut through the woods to get to his aunts' house.

"Nick," said a bodiless voice.

"GAAAAH!" Nick immediately teleported three times in rapid succession, stopping only when he'd smacked his head on a low branch and fell to the ground. He felt a hand around his wrist but saw no one.

"I'm sorry." The bus driver's voice was close to him. "I'm very, very sorry. I did not mean to frighten you."

"You. Are. Invisible." Nick said, trying not to hyperventilate. "Do we need to put a bell on you or something?"

"It's not a terrible idea," Ed said, helping Nick up. "That's quite the . . . talent you have."

"I don't know if I'd call it a talent," Nick said, brushing the dirt and leaves off his clothes. "Playing the guitar well is a talent. I'm a freak."

"I know how you feel."

"At least no one sees you being a freak."

Ed sighed. "True enough. Look, is there nothing I can do to convince you to come to Philadelphia with us?"

Nick thought about what Farshad had said. On the one hand, they hardly knew Ed—Nick didn't even know his last name, and he wanted to take them all to some random doctor forty miles away from Muellersville. The whole thing sounded shady. On the other hand, two days ago he'd watched Ms. Zelle go all ninja badass and work with guys in hazmat suits to take Mr. Friend away, and no one had heard from him since. Nick was pretty sure he couldn't trust anyone.

"Look, man," he said in the general direction of where he thought Ed was. "My mom just got out of the hospital. She needs me. I'm not going to go to Philadelphia." He picked up his bag. "I'm sorry you're all invisible and that's got to be frustrating, but I just can't go."

"Dude. That dude is talking to himself." Paul Yoder and Sam Stoltzfus were walking through the trees toward Nick.

"Oh," Nick said. "Hi guys."

"Hey, lardo," Sam said. Of all the Farm Kids, Sam was the one Nick liked the least. Not that he liked any of them, but Sam had always been mean. One time he'd grabbed Jay and shoved his head into the toilet in the boys' room and flushed it repeatedly. He'd stopped because Jay kept laughing and yelling, "Again! Again!" but it was still a nasty thing to do.

Nick felt Ed's hand on his arm again, gently guiding him away from the Farm Kids. As he turned, a clump of dirt hit the side of his head. "Hey, lardbutt, I was talking to you!" Sam yelled.

Nick had always taken great pains to avoid dealing with the Farm Kids (as well as the Auxano Company Kids—it was better to just let them fight each other). He always figured that if he kept his head down and didn't annoy anyone he'd be fine. Sure, being Jay Carpenter's best friend made that difficult, but it was usually Jay who got noticed, Jay who had his head shoved into a toilet, and Jay who completely didn't care. No one really ever noticed Nick when Jay was around.

What would Jay do? Nick thought frantically. Jay would probably say something like "Hello my stout fellow, are we throwing earth now? Jolly good!" and gotten his butt kicked in a dirt-throwing fight.

"Just go," Nick heard Ed whisper. "I'll deal with them."

As Nick began to run, he heard Sam yelp, "Who threw that? Who threw that?"

Nick jerked his head back to see Paul getting a face full of dirt; Ed must have been throwing it at them from only a few feet away. Nick kept running until he reached the edge of the woods.

So what now? Did he owe Ed something for sticking up for him? But the Farm Kids would never have picked on him in the first place if he hadn't looked like he was talking to himself in the woods like a crazy person. So in a way, Ed owed it to Nick to have his back against those jerks. Right? Maybe?

Nick got to Molly and Jilly's house and dug his key out of his pocket. "Hey, sweaty!" Jilly said as he walked through the front door. "Your mom is sleeping. Want some juice or something?" She waddled to the fridge as Nick slumped into a stool at the breakfast bar. "We have . . . we have water. And seltzer."

"Water's fine," Nick wheezed, trying, somehow, to sweat less. Jilly brought him a glass and started to pour the water. Nick felt bad. "You really shouldn't be getting me stuff," he said. "I should be getting you stuff."

Jilly laughed. "I'm pregnant, not ill," she said, putting the pitcher back into the fridge.

"Yeah, but you're enormous," Nick said, holding the cold glass of water to his sweaty forehead.

"You've been through all manner of trauma lately, so I'm going to pretend that you didn't say that," Jilly told him.

"Sorry," Nick said sheepishly. "Has Mom been asleep long?"

"Nah, she's been up and down," Jilly said, pouring herself a glass of water. "Although I don't think it's because she's sick, mind you, I think she's just living the dream of napping as often as she'd like."

"Jealous?"

"Totally." Nick smiled. Jilly had been complaining about being too big to sleep properly for months. "So," she continued, "how are you holding up?"

"Fine."

"Ugh, you really are becoming a teenager. That was the most teenagery answer you could have possibly given." Jilly took some Girl Scout cookies out of the freezer. She and Molly froze everything. "I'm going to eat a bunch of these and say it's because the baby needs to eat Thin Mints, and if you want any you're going to tell me how you're really doing after you were in a major bus accident and then your house caught on fire. Mmmmmm. Minty. Chocolatey . . ."

"Okay!" Nick said, laughing and grabbing a cookie out of the cold sleeve. "I'm a little spacey," he admitted. "I kind of don't know what to do with myself. Everyone seems to expect me to act normal, like nothing happened, but I keep thinking about everything that happened."

"That *is* normal," Jilly said.

"I guess."

"So how do you want people to act?"

"I don't know. I'm just confused by why all this stuff happened to me." Nick couldn't help thinking about his dad, and he felt a lump forming in his throat. It made swallowing the cookie difficult. "I mean, enough already, right?"

Jilly put her hand on his. "Right."

"But then there are kids whose homes have been bombed and they're refugees and all they've ever known is gone, so I should really just deal, right?"

"Oh honey," Jilly said, "you're not really being fair to yourself. It's nice to have perspective but not if it shuts down the part of yourself that allows you to feel things."

"Are you finishing the Thin Mints?" Molly asked, entering the kitchen and staring at the half-empty box. "I thought I hid those."

"The baby wanted them!" Jilly exclaimed. Molly rolled her eyes.

"And I'm going through a bunch of stuff," Nick said.

"Ugh, you two are the worst. Is Angela still sleeping? We're supposed to meet with the insurance guy at the house in half an hour." Molly headed up the stairs to the guest room.

Jilly looked at Nick. "Never feel bad about feeling bad, okay? You're having an exceptionally crummy week. It's okay to let yourself feel rotten for a little while. And it's a great excuse to order pizza tonight and watch old *Buffy* episodes and make Molly get stuff for us because she feels bad."

Nick smiled and shook his head. "You're diabolical."

"Whatever. If she wants to be the one who gets pregnant the next time I'm sure that I'll be running around taking care of everything. Come on." Jilly waddled around the breakfast bar and stretched out her arms. "Hugs!"

Nick leaned in awkwardly and felt the baby kick him through Jilly's extended torso. "Hey!" he yelped.

"Your cousin loooooooves you!"

Nick's mom came down the stairs with Molly. She looked tired and pale. "Hey, sweetie." She leaned in for a hug. "Do you have a lot of homework?"

"Not too much. I can go with you to the house."

"You've got the exam to study for." Nick's mom picked up her purse and looked around. "Where's Jay?"

"Mom, he doesn't go everywhere with me." Jilly and Molly snorted in unison and the doorbell rang.

"My dearest Angela!" Jay exclaimed, bounding into the house and giving Nick's mom a fervent hug. That guy's timing never failed to astound.

"Hi, Jay. Okay, we're out. You two study, okay?"

"Oh yes," Jay said conspiratorially. "The old man and I have much to discuss."

I can't believe Nick and Farshad aren't coming.

Nick wants to be there for his mother.

And how is he going to be there for her when he accidentally transports himself into a refrigerator door?

Well, he'd still be close by.

Everything you say is disconcerting. Everything.

WHILE COOKIE DID NOT KNOW PHILADELPHIA like the back of her hand, she knew that the area of West Philadelphia where Dr. Gabriel Deery worked was not a particularly nice one. For one, it was underneath an elevated train track. Two, it was between two boarded-up storefronts. Three, it was in a boarded-up storefront that used to be a halal butcher shop.

"So . . . this is gross and we're going to be murdered," Cookie observed.

Martina looked up at the building, her eyes a deep blue. "No, it's going to be okay."

She always spoke as if she knew things that the rest of them didn't know. It was disconcerting, but at the same time oddly calming. In a way it was nice that someone wasn't freaking out, because Abe looked like he was about to have a panic attack. Some men hanging out at the bottom of the stairs to the train platform were looking at them, and Cookie was pretty sure that if the men took one step toward them Abe was going to pass out.

Ed knocked on the door to the butcher shop. After a moment a man appeared from inside to let them in.

Dr. Deery led them through the abandoned butcher shop to a flight of stairs, and Cookie felt a sudden urge to hold someone's hand. Abe would probably flinch so hard that he'd fall down the stairs or barf or spontaneously combust.

Martina, as usual, had her hands full with her sketchbook and pen. If Nick had come along Cookie could have held on to him under the guise of keeping him safe; that would have been good. Farshad probably wouldn't have wanted her touching him—he'd made it pretty clear that she wasn't his favorite person. Cookie swallowed hard and followed the scientist down the stairs.

Cookie had been to her mom's office at Auxano plenty of times. Of course her mom worked in the accounting department, and not in one of the labs, but based on what Cookie had seen of the company headquarters she could easily imagine that their labs were well-lit, clean, sleek, organized, and pretty much everything that Dr. Deery's lab wasn't.

There were a few bolted-down metal tables in the center of a large room with low ceilings. Were they tables that had been used to butcher animals? Cookie tried to keep her disgust from showing on her face.

In the corner of the room were several cages with white rats in them. The lab smelled like a combination of chemicals and a cat-hoarder's kitchen.

"I'm sorry it's such a mess," Dr. Deery said, eyeing them warily. "Ed, I don't know where I'm supposed to look."

"I'm right here," Ed's voice sounded from near the rat cages.

"Extraordinary," Dr. Deery said, and turned to look at Cookie. "You must be Daniesha Parker. And you," he said, turning to Martina, "are Martina Saltis." Martina's eyes turned a silvery gray. Dr. Deery ran his hand through his messy hair, tugging it a little in the back like a nervous tic. "Simply astonishing."

"And you," he continued, looking at Abe. "You, too, have been affected?"

"I'm not sure," Abe said nervously.

"Yes, you are," Cookie said. "Go show him." She pointed to the cages of rats.

Abe looked at her with a mixture of irritation, curiosity, and fear. She glared back, and he moved toward the rat cages. The rodents turned to look at him. "Please lay down," he told them, and all at once they flopped onto their sides. Dr. Deery rushed to the cages.

"Are they alive?" he asked breathlessly.

"Yes, of course," Abe said. "It's okay to get back up if you want," he said to the rats, who got back up and watched him expectantly.

"Can you make them jump?" Martina asked.

"Probably," Abe said, "but that seems sort of rude. They probably don't want to jump."

Cookie snorted. "Well, we wouldn't want to be rude."

"Can they talk to you?" Dr. Deery asked.

"No, they're rats," Abe said, looking at the scientist as if his question was completely absurd.

Cookie pressed her fingers to her temples. She could hear the sounds of people outside thinking about how to get up to the train platform and it was making it hard for her to have her own thoughts. She took a deep breath. "Dr. Deery. Please tell us what's going on. And what we can do to make it stop."

"Of course, of course," Dr. Deery said, and gestured to

a beat-up sofa near the rat cages. It looked as if he'd been using it to sleep on. "Please sit down.

"It started a few years ago when I was working at the Auxano labs," he began as they sat down (after making certain that no one accidentally squished Ed). "I was in charge of a project that involved the artificial chemical enhancement of leporidae mental capacity."

"Say what now?" Cookie asked.

"They were trying to make bunnies smarter." Ed explained.

"Why? Why would anyone do that?" Abe asked.

"We were working on creating a drug, phlebotinum, that would help humans with borderline IQs to improve their cognitive functions. That was the idea." Dr. Deery said. "And we were using rabbits as test subjects."

"So you were trying to make dumb people smart," Cookie said.

"No, no. I was trying to make rabbits smart," Dr. Deery said. "If the drugs had worked we might have tried to develop them for people who had been mentally incapacitated by accidents or birth defects or childhood lead poisoning . . . but I was years away from that sort of practical application. We were just doing tests on rabbits."

"Did the rabbits become very smart?" Martina asked. She was drawing a rabbit with glasses and a pipe. Cookie started to ask her why a smart rabbit would be smoking a pipe, but thought better of it.

"That's very clever," Dr. Deery said, looking at Martina's sketchbook. She looked up at him, her eyes changing from brown to an icy blue. He took a step back, clearly unnerved. "I'm so sorry about what's happened to you all," he said.

"And what exactly happened to us?" Cookie asked.

Dr. Deery composed himself. "The experiments on the rabbits weren't going well—none of my formulas seemed to garner any results. One time I thought that a rabbit was getting smarter, but I suspect that it was just a smarter rabbit to begin with. Then one night I was working by myself when one of my overhead lights went out.

"I should have called maintenance, but I thought I could just replace the fluorescent bulb without having to bother anyone. Long story short, I accidentally electrocuted the rabbit enclosure."

"You killed the bunnies?"

"No! No, they seemed fine." Dr. Deery sat on a stool and eyed the rats. "But they had changed."

"Were they like us?" Martina asked.

"No, not exactly. Their eyes didn't change color, there was no teleportation, none of them turned invisible . . ." Dr. Deery's voice trailed off and he looked pale. "At least, I don't think any of them turned invisible . . ."

"What happened to them?" Cookie steeled herself for possible horrible bunny fates. "Did they explode? Eat each other?"

"They got really loud."

Cookie looked at Abe, who seemed confused, and then at Martina, who had a skeptical look on her face. "Loud?" she asked.

"Yes, loud. But *really* loud. They started screaming and burst my lab assistant's eardrums," Dr. Deery explained. "It was unbearably loud. We had to evacuate the floor and outfit ourselves with noise-cancelling headphones before we could return to the lab and take care of the rabbits."

"Take care of them?" Cookie asked with raised eyebrows. "Did you kill them?"

Dr. Deery shook his head vigorously. "No, no, we merely sedated them and began to take blood samples for further study. We knew that we had stumbled onto something major, we just didn't know what.

"Unfortunately," he went on, "shutting down the entire floor until we were able to get the rabbits under control got the attention of the Auxano administrators. They were fascinated with the potential practical applications of my work with phlebotinum."

"Practical applications?" Cookie asked.

"We'd taken normal, everyday rabbits and—accidentally, it should be noted—given them abilities far beyond anything that normal rabbits would be able to do."

"Rabbits don't usually scream," Abe said knowingly.

"No, they don't, and they certainly don't scream loud enough to injure anyone. Humans aren't able to scream loud enough to truly injure someone. We'd stumbled upon something huge, and the higher-ups at Auxano knew it.

"For months we ran tests on the rabbits, and the data we collected was fascinating." Dr. Deery looked wistful. "I could have studied those rabbits for the rest of my professional career. But we were getting pressure from the administrators to recreate the circumstances that enhanced the rabbits in the first place."

"They wanted more screaming bunnies?" Cookie asked.

"They wanted to move the process forward to human subjects."

Martina stopped drawing to look up at Dr. Deery. Her eyes flashed from gray to blue to brown to a lighter blue before settling back on gray. Cookie wondered for the hundredth time what it was that triggered the changes in Martina's eye color. Was she upset? Angry? Was it all just random? Cookie stood up from her place on the sofa, moved to Martina, and put her arms around her. In the short time that they'd known each other, Cookie had gotten the impression that the strange girl wasn't really a hugger, but Cookie needed to feel grounded.

Martina leaned in, ever so slightly, to Cookie's hug. Whatever was going on, they were in it together.

"Are we test subjects?" Cookie asked in a low voice.

"No, no." Dr. Deery looked miserable. "No, you're not. You're . . . accidents."

"Explain. Now."

"First, the experiments were never supposed to result in"—Dr. Deery gestured to everyone—"all this. The goal was to create a drug that could be used to boost preexisting

IQs, not create entirely new abilities. Second, I was against repeating the experiment until we had all the data, and vehemently against using human subjects. My employers seemed to back off, but they kept adding new people to my team that I had never before worked with. I grew suspicious and discovered that samples of my original formula were missing. My assistant suspected that someone was copying our files. I began to keep copies of my research data on an external hard drive that I kept in my car.

"One Friday night I came back to the lab after hours. I had left my brother's birthday present in my office and his party was the next day, so I went back to pick it up. Then I heard two of my new lab cohorts speaking in the hallway. I was about to ask them what they were still doing there so late when I heard them talk about 'resistant test subjects.' I followed them instead.

"They didn't go to the lab that we were sharing. They instead descended into a basement room that I had never seen before. I watched through the window of the lab door as they put eye drops of what looked like my phlebotinum into a drinking glass of water, and then put a straw into the glass. They were clearly going to give it to a person. I was horrified."

He was quiet for a moment. "I copied the rest of my files to the external hard drive and brought it to Ed to hide in case anything happened to me. Then I erased the rest of my research from my work computer and my home computer."

There was a dry laugh from the corner of the sofa. "And yet you never gave me my birthday present."

"I didn't? Oh, I didn't. It was a 3-D puzzle of a globe."

"Oh, I would have enjoyed that." Ed sounded a little bummed.

"Guys," Cookie said. "Who were they testing the phlebotinum on?"

"We don't know." Dr. Deery said. "I called my supervisor at her house on Saturday morning and told her what I'd seen. She told me that I was probably just jumping to conclusions but she promised me that she'd look into it. On Monday when I came back to work I was immediately called to her office and fired, and then they had a security guard watch me as I packed up my personal things. I wasn't even allowed to say good-bye to anyone.

"When I got back to my apartment I found that it had been ransacked. My computer was stolen, along with all of my CDs and thumb drives. Every drawer had been opened, every framed picture had been taken off the wall and thrown to the floor. They went so far as to slash the cushions of my sofa and my mattress. I gathered as much of my things as I could, threw them in the car, and drove here.

"This building belonged to our uncle . . ." Dr. Deery continued. "I've tried to continue my research," he said, gesturing to the lab equipment and the rats, "but I lost a lot. Up until about a week ago I felt reassured that at least the scientists at Auxano didn't have my files. But they did have the samples of the formula, as well as the infected rabbits."

"That's where I thought I could help," Ed said. It was always a little startling to hear him chime in when he hadn't spoken for a while. Cookie wondered for a moment what would happen if he wore a hat. "Gabe had got me a gig as a night security guard at the company a while back."

"I thought you were a bus driver," Martina said.

"Yes, but only part-time. I needed to make ends meet. I'm really a sculptor."

"He's very good," Dr. Deery said.

"Thanks Gabe, that's nice to hear."

"FOCUS, NERDS!" Cookie said.

"Sorry," Dr. Deery said quickly. "I asked Ed if he could get the phlebotinum for me. I wanted to run tests on it so I could have evidence not only that I had been fired unfairly and my work had been stolen from me, but that it was being used for ethically questionable purposes. The night before your field trip he was able to break into the lab and take it."

"Weren't you worried that they'd suspect you?" Martina asked in the direction of the sofa.

"A little. But no one at Auxano knew that we were brothers." Ed explained. "Technically we're half brothers, which is why we have different last names. Plus no one would ever think an artist would be smart enough to know what to take," he added. "Or a bus driver."

"He did a great job of finding the phlebotinum and getting it here. The bus trip was a nice cover. The only problem is that he did a little too good of a job." Dr. Deery said.

"I didn't understand that I was only supposed to bring a sample." Ed said sheepishly.

"He brought all of it." Dr. Deery said. "When I saw what he'd brought I was tempted to keep it all. Now I wish I did. But I took a little bit and told him to take the rest back so that no one would realize it was missing. I was afraid he'd be found out and arrested for taking the stuff."

"They must know now that you took it," Cookie said.

"They do," Ed said with a heavy sigh. "My apartment and my studio were completely upended, but of course they couldn't find anything because it was all in the bus accident."

"I'm fairly sure that they were able to retrieve what was left from the bus before the police could investigate." Dr. Deery said. "These are very powerful people with a lot of money. The only good thing about my brother's . . . current condition is that they can't find him. And I can't tell you how impressed I am that you guys have kept your own . . .

conditions to yourselves. There's no telling what the people at Auxano would do to you if they knew about your . . . skills."

Martina blinked. "But isn't that what we're here for? So that you can study what happened to us during the accident?"

"Yes, yes. I'm so sorry but I'm going to need blood samples from you. And hopefully eventually from Mr. Rajavi and Mr. Gross."

"And you'll be able to cure us?" Cookie asked.

"How . . . how will you get the blood?" Abe asked.

The vein is right here.

Hold. Still.

No no no no no noooo no no

THE DAILY WHUT?

Hey, intrepid minds, seekers of truths, and questioners of the status quo, has anyone seen Ryan Friend? The police haven't, and they also don't seem too worried about it, particularly in the light of the last fire, at the Zook farm out in Amish country.

Is it just me, or is it too much of a coincidence that the hired goons from our local economy gods Auxano were harassing our Plain brothers and sisters just a few months ago? You all remember my now eerily prophetic post about the Auxano Company cars seen coming and going from the Amish-owned farms in the area. At the time I suspected foul play, and I'm not happy to see that my suspicions were ALL BUT VERIFIED by the fire at the Zooks' last week.

Dear readers, SOMETHING IS UP. I'm not totally certain as to what it is just yet, but oh, I have IDEAS, and as we all know, sometimes those ideas become truths, like when I knew that Mayor Kirby was going to win the election even though the week before Election Day she was still eleven points behind in the polls. THAT ELECTION WAS RIGGED,

MY FRIENDS, and one day I'm going to prove it, just like
I'm going to prove that the events in Amish country had
something to do with the fires in town and Ryan Friend's
disturbing disappearance.

Until then, keep asking questions,
THE HAMMER

She had been with a few other friends on Rumspringa, and they were all acting strangely when they returned.

Everyone was worried. The elders in the community met with them to put them back on the right path.

No one talks about what happened at that meeting, but when it was over Rebecca and four of her friends had been shunned. We weren't supposed to know, but we heard that they had been accused of being Hexerei.

They had to leave their homes and we haven't heard from them since. If we do, we're not supposed to talk to them.

Hexes?

Witchcraft.

Yes.

Hold up. Do you seriously think your own sister is a witch?

I can tell rats to lie down and they listen to me. I don't know what to think.

SO DO YOU REALLY THINK YOUR BROTHER CAN HELP us?" Cookie asked, chewing on the soft pretzel they'd bought at the Wawa before leaving Philadelphia. She tried not to watch as Ed ate. The pretzel just sort of floated and then slowly disappeared. It was unnerving. Cookie found herself wondering if he made invisible poops, and was immediately grossed out by herself. Hanging out with all these oddballs was starting to rub off on her.

"I don't know," Ed said. "I don't want to make promises that we might not be able to keep. But he is brilliant, I know that much." "But you would say that," Cookie said. "He's your brother."

Cookie heard Ed sigh. "I get that you're skeptical. That's healthy. But before Auxano threw him out Gabe was completely on the straight and narrow. High school valedictorian, top of his class at Penn, prestigious scholarships to—" Ed muttered an explctive. "Abe, quickly, we have to trade places."

"Excuse me?" Abe asked, aghast. Cookie turned in her seat to see the flashing red and blue lights of a police car behind them. Ed was pulling over to the side of the road. "You have to get into the driver's seat NOW."

Put your hands flat on your lap. Cookie remembered her mother's instructions in the event of getting pulled over by the police. *Say nothing. Only speak if you're spoken to, and call the policeman "Sir" or "Officer," and whatever you do, never sass him. I'm serious.*

There was a brief and awkward tussle as Abe climbed over Ed to get into the front seat. "Strap in," Ed snapped.

"What? Where? How?" Abe looked like he was going to faint.

"Put on your seat belt," Martina explained.

"And put your hands on the wheel," Cookie hissed. "Never take your hands off the wheel. And open the window."

"How? How does it open?" Abe pressed his hands flat on the window, trying to push it down.

"Oh my god, we're all going to jail." Cookie groaned. They were only a few miles out of Muellersville. Maybe she could hurl herself out of the car and make a run for it? Probably a bad idea.

"Cookie, that's enough," Ed growled. Cookie could see Abe's chest flattening as Ed leaned over to open the window for him. "It's this switch. Just stay calm. Hands on the wheel. We're going to get through this."

"How?" Cookie asked as the police officer approached the driver's side of the car. She put her hands flat on her lap.

"License and registration." The police officer peered into the car. Abe looked like he was going to faint.

"Excuse me?" he asked.

"I said license. And. Registration." The glove compartment door popped open and Cookie watched as the car registration inched forward. She was terrified to say anything, but someone had to help Abe, and it certainly wasn't going to be Martina, who was drawing contentedly in her sketchbook as if they weren't all about to get arrested.

"Right there," Cookie said in what she hoped was an even voice. "The registration is where you left it right there in the glove compartment." Abe looked desperately lost. "The open car box."

The police officer eyed Cookie suspiciously and seemed to be on the verge of asking her a question when he let out a yelp. "AUGH!"

A bird had pooped right in the middle of his ticketing pad. "Oh, that's disgusting, excuse me," the officer grumbled, shaking out the pad. Another bird poop hit the brim of his hat. "AUGGGHHH!" Two poops landed on the officer's left shoulder, and then three on his right. A light gray glob of excrement dripped down his chest.

Cookie looked out the window. They were parked on the side of the road near open farmland, and a huge swarm of small birds was flying just above the car. Cookie looked at Abe, who was staring straight ahead with his hands firmly grasping the wheel.

"WHAT THE AUUUGGGHHH!!!" The police officer was now covered in bird poop that was falling from the sky like disgusting, bird-poopy hail. "JUST BE CAREFUL ON THE ROAD!" he screamed to Abe before sprinting back to his patrol car. Abe pushed the button that raised the window.

"Holy—" Cookie started.

"Good work, Abe," Ed interrupted her. "I think it's time you learned to use the windshield wipers."

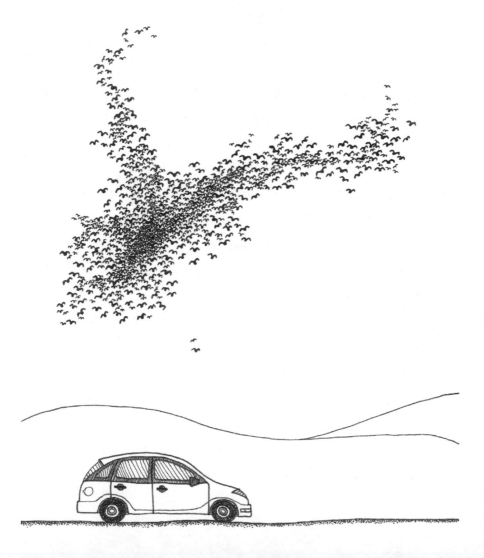

YOU DROPPED A WHAT ON MY COMPUTER?" FARSHAD'S dad looked more surprised than upset. That seemed like a good sign, right? Maybe? Farshad was really not accustomed to disappointing his parents. He really didn't know what to expect.

"The dictionary. I was looking something up, and it slipped out of my hands and fell on the keyboard."

"But why didn't you just look it up on the computer?" his dad asked. Farshad grimaced. He'd chosen the dictionary because it was the heaviest book he could think of, besides the *Complete Works of Shakespeare*, and he couldn't come up with a good reason to be reading the *Complete Works of Shakespeare*. Maybe he wanted to peruse *Macbeth*? Too late now.

"I wanted to see if the word *antidisestablishmentarianism* was in the actual dictionary," Farshad explained.

"But . . . why?"

"It's a really long word," Farshad explained weakly. "I wanted to see what it looked like on a paper page. I'm really sorry about the computer."

His dad looked sadly at the indented keyboard of the ruined laptop. "I'll take it into work to see if any of the tech guys have a solution. Don't worry, it's not your fault. Just be a little more careful next time. New rule! No dictionary reading over a laptop."

"Never again," Farshad promised. If he kept accidentally crushing things with his super-thumbs he was going to have to come up with some new and more plausible explanations. Maybe he could ask Cookie for help. She seemed good at that sort of thing.

Farshad blinked, wondering at the circumstances that had led him to thinking positively about any aspect of Cookie Parker's personality (and considering that being an easy liar was one of her attractive qualities).

Farshad's mother came into the room. "Arastoo, did you tell him about the trip?"

"What trip?" Farshad asked.

"Your teacher called us," Farshad's mother said excitedly, "to ask for permission to go on a special Science Club field trip next week to the lab. Ms. Zelle," she added, and Farshad felt the hairs on the back of his neck stand up. Dr. Rajavi turned to spot the ruined laptop for the first time. "What happened here?" she asked.

"He accidentally dropped a dictionary on the computer," Farshad's father explained.

"What was he using a dictionary for?"

"Why did Ms. Zelle call you?" Farshad asked. "Why didn't she just tell me and send home a permission slip?"

"Oh, she explained," Dr. Rajavi said. "She wanted permission to take a sample of your blood so they can show you the big centrifuge and map your very own DNA—it's a great opportunity for you and your group!"

Farshad swallowed nervously. "I was looking up the word *antidisestablishmentarianism*," he told her. His mother stared at him blankly. "That's why I was using the dictionary. I wanted to look up *antidisestablishmentarianism*."

"Oh," she said. "Well, let's be more careful in the future." Farshad caught her shooting a quick look to his father. They were clearly confused. "Aren't you excited about the trip to Auxano?" his mother asked.

"Yes!" Farshad bleated, and took a breath. "Yes. Of course. I'm just upset about the computer."

Farshad's dad came up to him and put his arm around his shoulder. "That's okay, it's just a computer. I'm sure the guys at work will fix it up in no time. They love a challenge."

"Are you all right, Farshad?" his mother asked.

"Sure," Farshad said. "I'm fine."

"I heard you up a few nights ago," she said, concerned. "You were up when you should have been sleeping."

"I was just studying for the exam," he lied.

"Of course, of course," Dr. Rajavi said, but she looked worried. "Are you hungry? Have you eaten?"

"I'm okay," he said, carefully gathering up his things. "But I could use a run before it gets dark."

"Go, go."

Farshad went to his room and changed into gym shorts and a T-shirt. It was still a little chilly out but the cold was good—it usually made him run faster. Farshad set off on one of his usual routes. Down to the end of the street, up the path through the woods, by the creek, past the park and to the school. He ran without thinking, which was why he was very surprised to find himself standing outside Cookie Parker's house. She was sitting on her front step and look-ing at her phone. She looked up at him, surprised.

"You got my email?" she asked. "I just sent it."

"No," he replied. "My computer kind of broke. I was just out for a run." How had he ended up outside her house? It was not on his usual route.

"Oh," she said. "I just wrote to tell you that I wanted to meet up for a study group . . ." She looked around, slightly nervous, and continued in a quieter voice. "But I wanted to tell you what we found out in Philadelphia. Let's go inside."

Farshad did not want to go into Cookie Parker's house. Sitting and talking about all the bizarre things that were threatening to overtake his life was exactly what he'd been trying to avoid by not going to Philadelphia with her in the first place. But he felt compelled to follow her inside anyway.

Cookie's house looked like his, only with more framed photos on the walls instead of small Oriental rugs. Farshad looked at a family photo and tried to hide his surprise at seeing that her dad was white.

"He's my stepfather," Cookie said, leading Farshad into the kitchen.

"Did you just hear my thoughts?" Farshad gaped. Were her powers growing?

Cookie snorted. "No, I saw that you were looking at the photo and you had that *Oh my god, she's half-white* look on your face. I see it every time I go out to dinner with my parents," she added with a roll of her eyes.

"Sorry," Farshad said sheepishly, and then felt slightly annoyed that he was apologizing for his thoughts. Maybe one day talking to Cookie Parker wouldn't leave him so conflicted.

She handed him a glass of water without asking if he wanted one, and he took it gratefully. She might not be able to read the minds of people who weren't thinking about directions, but she was perceptive. Farshad found himself wondering if their abilities were in any way related to preexisting personality traits; maybe Cookie's ability to (sort of) read minds was just an extension of her natural gift for reading people. But what did that mean for him? Super strength in his thumbs could be an extension of . . . he had no idea.

"So Ed took us to see his brother," Cookie started as Farshad drank his water, and told him about the dingy lab under the train tracks, the electrical accident at Auxano, and the formula that had turned them into supernatural freaks in the bus wreck. "Dr. Deery thinks that it's going to take some time but he might be able to figure out how to reverse whatever happened to us."

"And you trust him?" Farshad asked. "My parents work at Auxano, and I'm pretty sure they're not involved in any nefarious file-stealing or ransacking apartments."

"My parents work for Auxano, too," Cookie said defensively.

"So do you believe this guy?"

Cookie rubbed her temples. "I don't know. But so far he's the only one with any answers."

Farshad leaned back in his seat. "Fortune cookies have answers."

Cookie sat up and gave him a hard look. "Do you have any answers?"

"What about asking Auxano?"

"You're kidding."

"No, I'm not. Why don't we just go to Auxano and have them figure it out?"

"Were you listening at all to the story I just told you?" Cookie looked aghast. "They stole Dr. Deery's research, fired him, and ransacked his apartment. They're not exactly trustworthy."

"And he is? You just met him! But I've known my parents for, oh, my entire life, and you've known your parents for roughly as long and I don't know about you, but I've never seen my parents do anything worse than accidentally park their car in a handicapped spot. And they felt bad about it. Why are we suddenly trusting Dr. Dirty Lab over our own parents?"

Cookie looked furious. "I'm sorry, but were you not at the barn? Did you not see what happened to Mr. Friend?"

"And what did happen to him?" Farshad asked. Cookie was standing now, so he stood up, too. "He was a dangerously unhinged man who was lighting stuff on fire with his mind, and people who could handle him took him to a place where he couldn't hurt anyone else. I, for one, support that action."

"Oh, and would you be supportive if it happened to one of us? What if they took me away to 'a place where I couldn't hurt anyone else'? Is that what you want?"

"Well . . ."

"Oh my god. Shut up. Do you want to be taken to some place where you can't hurt anyone with your . . . thumbs?"

"Well, maybe they would have been nicer about helping him if he hadn't been so crazy. Maybe if he'd been able to approach them and say, 'Hey guys, I've been accidentally lighting stuff on fire with my mind, a little help?' they might not have had to take him by force."

"So is that what you want to do? Go to Auxano and say, 'Hi! I'm a great big freak! Help me!'"

"I don't know. Maybe? I just don't think that we should immediately trust a disgraced and possibly mad scientist and his weird bus-driving invisible brother."

"He's a sculptor! Driving the bus is his day job." Cookie snarled.

"Wait, is that supposed to convince me that he's aboveboard? That he's a sculptor?" Farshad sniped back.

"No, I just thought it was INTERESTING."

"Hey, Cooks, what's happening here?" A tall white man with thinning hair walked into the kitchen and stood next to Cookie while appraising Farshad with a wary eye.

"Hi, George," Cookie said. "This is Farshad."

Farshad extended his hand awkwardly to Cookie's stepfather. "Hello, Mr. Parker, it's nice to meet you," he said.

"Actually, it's Mr. MacKessy," Cookie's stepfather replied coolly, shaking Farshad's hand with a little too much grip. Farshad took care not to reciprocate, not wanting to break every bone in the man's hand despite the fact that Mr. MacKessy was looking at him with suspicion. Farshad understood. It's not every day you see a tall brown dude hanging out in your house alone with your daughter.

"Sorry, Mr. MacKessy," Farshad said, taking his hand back. "Cookie and I were just—"

"Farshad was just leaving," Cookie said, shooting Farshad a look that was clearly telling him to Shut. Up.

"I was just leaving," Farshad said, picking up his empty water glass to put it in the kitchen sink. It shattered in his hand. "Oh my gosh, I am so sorry . . ."

"Don't worry, don't worry," Mr. MacKessy said quickly, grabbing the remaining shards from Farshad's hand and putting them on the kitchen counter. "Are you hurt? Are you bleeding?"

Farshad looked down at his hand. Not a scratch, of course. "No, I'm fine," he said.

"Come over to the sink, let's put your hand under the light to get a better look," Mr. MacKessy said worriedly.

"George, he said he was fine," Cookie said, grabbing a broom and a dustpan. "You're fine, right?"

"Yeah," Farshad said. "I'm so sorry about the glass."

"He's got to go now."

"But I've got to go."

"But we'll talk later."

"Sure," Farshad said noncommittally, and headed out the door to run and not think some more.

LET ME READ IT AGAIN," JAY SAID, SNATCHING COOKIE'S note from Nick's fingers and leaning back against the wall in the Understeps. "Look at her handwriting." He sighed. "It's exquisite."

"Really?" Nick asked, looking over Jay's shoulder at the three pages that described what Cookie and Martina had learned from Dr. Deery. "It looks kind of sloppy to me."

"Look at the lines," Jay said dreamily. "She writes with power. She's not afraid of the paper."

"Okeydokey." Nick watched Jay pore over what Cookie had written. She had explained first that Ed had told her to stop using the Internet to talk about their new abilities in case someone was hacking their email. From the look of her note, Cookie had become increasingly irritated with having to use an actual pen and paper. By the time she'd gotten to the part of the story where Abe's sister was shunned from the Amish community, Cookie's handwriting was almost illegible. Still, Nick was grateful for the update. "So what do you think?" he asked Jay.

"The ending is a little harder to read," Jay admitted.

"No, what do you think about the actual story?"

"Ah. Yes. FASCINATING. We have a lot to think about. I wish I had gone with them—if you all go back to Dr. Deery's lab I'm going to insist that I accompany you."

"I don't see them going back any time soon."

"They might not, but you ought to. He should have a sample of your blood as well."

"Should he?" Nick turned around to see Farshad ducking his head underneath the stairwell to join them.

"Did Cookie give you one of these, too?" Nick asked him, gesturing to the note that Jay was reading again.

"No, she told me the story when I saw her yesterday."

"Wait, were we supposed to meet up yesterday to talk?" Nick felt a surge of the all too familiar sensation of being left out.

"No, I was just out for a run yesterday and saw her, so she told me everything."

"Oh," Nick said, slightly unnerved by his own relief. "So, what do you think?"

Farshad leaned against the wall. He looked grim. "Look, I asked my parents about Dr. Deery last night."

Jay looked up from the note, his eyes wide. "Did you tell them about your power?"

"No, not yet. I just made it sound like I heard a rumor about him. They told me that he'd been fired for unethical experiments, and they seemed to think that he was pretty crazy."

"And you believed them?" Nick asked.

"My own parents? Yeah, I believed my own parents. And after hearing about how Dr. Deery is working from some nasty butcher-shop basement, I'm thinking that my gainfully employed scientist parents are a lot more trustworthy than he is." Farshad sighed and picked up his backpack. "Don't worry, I'm not going to tell anyone anything yet. For all we know, these . . . powers . . . could just go away if we drink a lot of water. But if stuff gets worse I'm going to tell my folks and see what the people at Auxano have to say."

"You can't do that," Jay said. "It's not just your secret to tell!"

"And it's not yours at all." Farshad snapped. "Look, we're going to be late to class."

"Okay, just . . . let's talk about this later?" Nick asked.

"Yeah, maybe." Farshad walked away.

"There goes a young man with many issues," Jay mused. "But don't worry, he's not going to tell his parents."

"Oh?" Nick asked, gathering up his own things. "And what makes you so certain of that?"

"Because we're going to get to the truth of the matter."

"With our renowned sleuthing skills?" Nick asked.

"Do you really think they're renowned? I did find the missing class hamster in fifth grade."

"Jay, you're the one who let Sir Nutcheeks out of the cage."

"Of course I did. He needed to feel, even for the briefest of times, the sweetness of freedom and self-determination.

We've been over this." Jay leapt to his feet. "We're going to find Mr. Friend."

"No, we're going to go to class," Nick said, heading down the hallway to their homeroom. He honestly didn't know what the next step was, but he knew that the exam was the next day, and the one thing that he could control was being in the classroom to take it. Unless he blinked out during the middle of the test . . .

Nick felt Jay's hand on his elbow. "I just did it, didn't I?" Nick asked.

Jay nodded. "Let's take deep, healing breaths and head to class, shall we?"

"Hey, look, it's Fatboy and his boyfriend," Nick heard a voice behind him. Farm Kids. Great.

Jay turned around, keeping his hand on Nick. "Are you talking about us?" he asked Sam and Paul.

"I don't see anyone else here," Sam sneered, looking around.

"Well, while I would be lucky to have a boyfriend as thoughtful and kind as my friend Nick here, alas, we are not romantically linked." Jay explained, "At this point in my development I mostly identify as heterosexual."

Sam looked confused. "See," he said, "I told you he was gay."

"No, no, my poor, dim friend, 'heterosexual' means that

I'm attracted to people of the opposite sex. That means women," Jay said.

"We should go," Nick said, grabbing his nonromantic friend and steering him toward their first class. Jay would stay in the hallway explaining the difference between homosexuality and heterosexuality until Sam and Paul shoved him into a locker.

"Bye, lover boys," Sam yelled down the hall after them.

"You misunderstand," Jay said as Nick dragged him away. "We're really just good friends. I'm deeply in love with Daniesha . . ."

Nick could hear them laughing as they left. His face burned with frustrated anger, not because he cared what they thought but because they'd made being gay sound like something shameful. He should have spoken up. What if Molly and Jilly had been there? All he could do was stand like a big goober and be terrified of Jay letting go of him and him accidentally transporting himself into a brick wall of the hallway.

"Cheer up, old boy," Jay said. "We'll get to the bottom of everything that's happening. Everything will become much clearer after we find Mr. Friend, I promise."

Nick was not particularly comforted.

COOKIE GOT TO MRS. WHITAKER'S CLASS EARLY. Well, early for Cookie, in that she didn't run in right as the bell was sounding. There was absolutely no way that she was ending up in the back of a class again with Yokel McRacistjerk. She wasn't particularly sure about how the Farm Kids felt about Asians but was completely willing to let Emma Lee find out.

"Hello, Cookie," Mrs. Whitaker said, "good to see you. How are you feeling?"

"Just fine, thanks," Cookie said, doing her best to not look guarded.

"Your head is all healed?" Mrs. Whitaker asked.

"Sure," Cookie said. "Good as new." Addison and Claire walked into the room and sat down next to Cookie. Emma Lee followed and sat behind her.

"Is anyone feeling nervous about the exam?" Mrs. Whitaker asked.

"Definitely me," Emma said, giggling. What a lie. That girl aced every exam and everyone knew it. Cookie suppressed the urge to roll her eyes.

"Oh, I'm sure you'll be fine," Mrs. Whitaker said, turning around to start writing on the whiteboard.

"Where were you?" Claire hissed to Cookie.

"Where was I when?" Cookie asked as the rest of the class filed in. Sam Stoltzfus headed toward her. She made herself look bored and he sneered as he walked by her desk.

"Yesterday! We were supposed to be studying together!" Claire was getting hyped up.

"Girl, chill," Cookie said. "I had family stuff."

"Are you even ready?" Addison asked from her other side. "We went over A LOT. Emma's notes are *extensive*."

"I'm sure I'll do just fine without Emma's . . ." Cookie's voice trailed off.

Must get her out of class. Must separate her from the rest of them.

Look normal. Act like nothing is a big deal.

Just get Cookie alone.

Cookie heard Ms. Zelle's voice in her head as clearly as if she had been sitting right next to her, but the science teacher was nowhere to be seen.

"Cookie?" Addison asked. "Earth to Cookie. Come in, Cookie."

"God, you're so spacey," Claire said.

"I have to go," Cookie said, standing up quickly and walking to the front of the class. "Mrs. Whitaker, I've got to go."

"I thought you said you were fine."

"I'm not. I've got to go." *Look normal*, Cookie told herself. "I think I just need a moment to splash some water in my face. I'll be right back," she added, before Mrs. Whitaker could respond, and darted out the door and around the corner. She immediately opened an empty locker and hid behind the door as Ms. Zelle rounded the corner and went into Mrs. Whitaker's room. Cookie could hear Ms. Zelle asking where she was. Cookie walked quickly toward the Understeps.

"Where are we going?" Martina asked. It was as if she had appeared out of nowhere.

"GAH!" Cookie yelped.

"We should probably be quieter," Martina warned. "We did leave class again."

"What . . . how did you know I left class?" Cookie's heart was racing a million miles an hour.

"Because I saw you leaving. Where are we going?"

"Were you in the class?"

"Sure."

"How did you get out?"

"I just followed you."

"And no one noticed? How?"

Martina shrugged. "No one ever notices me. So why did you run out?"

Cookie steered Martina to the Understeps. No one important ever seemed to go there—it was as good a place as any to hide out.

"I heard her," Cookie whispered to Martina. "Ms. Zelle. I heard her coming to the class to find me." Cookie tapped her temple with her finger. "In here."

"Really?" Martina looked momentarily confused. "Why was she thinking about how to get to Mrs. Whitaker's class? She's been by it enough times."

"That's the thing—she wasn't thinking about how to get there. Ms. Zelle was thinking about how to get me out of there." Cookie took a deep breath. "I heard her thinking about how she had to separate me from everyone else and how she had to act normal. I had to get out before she got there."

"That does not seem good. She knows about you," Martina said.

"Do you think that's it?"

"Why else would she want to speak to you alone?" Martina asked.

"But why wouldn't she also be looking for you?" Cookie snapped.

"No one ever looks for me," Martina said matter-of-factly.

"Ugh, you're so weird," Cookie said. Her eyes widened as she heard someone coming down the steps above them. She grabbed Martina's arm and dragged her farther back underneath the stairs and raised her finger to her lips.

102

EXAM DAY!" NICK OPENED HIS EYES TO SEE JAY SITTING on the edge of the futon that Molly and Jilly had put in their newly set-up nursery. "Are you ready?"

"Boundaries," Nick groaned into his pillow. Holding an exam on a Saturday was too cruel.

Jay bounded over to the crib and started batting at a mobile of hanging farm animals. "Fascinating," he said.

"Stop that," Molly barked, poking her head into the room. "What are you, a cat?"

"But why barnyard animals?" Jay asked. "Is your baby going to be a farmer? Is it really so necessary to know about sheep and cows? People seem to believe that babies need to know all about sheep and cows."

"And ducks," Molly said. "Knowing about ducks is very important to child development."

"It is?"

"No, doofus, they're just cute and fluffy. Didn't I tell you to wait downstairs while I woke Nick up?"

"You did, my dear lady, but I decided to take it upon myself to help you as you have your hands full with taking care of your beautiful, child-laden wife."

"Boundaries!" Nick growled.

"Nicky, get up and get ready, it's exam day," Molly said. "Jay, GET OUT and go back to the kitchen."

"Would you mind terribly much if I partook of some coffee?"

"Oh no no no," Nick heard Molly say as she marched Jay down the stairs. "Angela already told me that you're not to have any caffeine."

"This is an outrage!"

Nick hauled himself off the rocky futon. His mom had told him that their house would be ready for them to move back into "soon," although she hadn't specified when exactly. He loved his aunts, but he missed sleeping in his own bed.

Exam Day. Nick had been dreading it for months, but the events of the past week had distracted him from the nausea that usually accompanied the threat of an upcoming test. It wasn't that he was stupid—Nick didn't consider himself to be a genius, but he could take one look at Farm Kids like Sam Stoltzfus and know that he at least wasn't a complete idiot—but he wasn't good at taking tests. Sitting in a big quiet room with only the sounds of pencils filling out answer bubbles made him incredibly nervous, and he was always second-guessing his answers. Time itself was Nick's enemy during tests—he'd look at the clock and realize that he didn't have much time left, and then he'd freak out and not be able to concentrate on answering the questions that were left, so he told himself not to look at the clock but then of course he was constantly looking at the clock and then worrying that he was losing time checking the time . . . Nick looked over and realized that he'd moved about a foot to his left just thinking about taking the test.

Oh no. Oh no no no. He was going to be in a crowded testing room and he completely couldn't stop himself from transporting. He did it again. "JAY!" He yelled, terrified, and then tried to breathe. "Jay," he called again.

Jay bounded back into the room. That kid was fast. "Jay, I'm freaking out," Nick explained, taking a big step to his right and immediately blinking back four inches to his left. "I don't think I can take this test!" He did it again.

Jay jumped forward and grabbed his arm. "Okay, okay, old man, breathe. In through the nose, out through the mouth. You must find your inner yogi. Waheguru."

"What are you talking about?"

"You know I've always been interested in Eastern spirituality! You are a rock. You are a mountain. You are a feather falling on a mountain. You are a drop of rain in the ocean! Just breathe."

Nick wasn't sure what Jay was talking about, but his weirdness was familiar and oddly calming. "Okay," he breathed. "I think I can go downstairs."

"Excellent! Jilly is making Molly cook crepes. Pregnant women get all the perks," Jay said.

Nick took another deep breath. "I don't know how I'm

going to get through this exam without teleporting," he told Jay.

Jay turned to face Nick and put both of his hands on Nick's arms. "Don't worry, old friend," he said seriously. "I will find a way to get you through this."

Intellectually Nick knew that putting his faith in the spazziest kid in school was probably not the best plan, but at least it was a plan.

THE EXAM WAS HELD IN THE CAFETERIA, WHICH ALWAYS struck Farshad as unnecessarily evil. He understood that it was easier for the team of proctors to oversee a larger room, and that it was more difficult to get away with cheating, but there was also the incessant humming of the vending machines, and if anyone sharpened their pencils the sound would reverberate throughout the entire room. Farshad found it annoying, although he could usually tune it out. He put his pencils on the table in front of him. One for answering the questions, a backup for if that one got dull, and two more backups for if he accidentally pulverized the first two.

Farshad tried not to seem like he was paying attention to his bus companions as they filed into the cafeteria. First there was Cookie, who looked as if she hadn't been sleeping very well. Farshad considered sending her an encouraging thought in the form of directions to the ice cream parlor, but decided against it. She probably had her brain full trying to ignore everyone else's thoughts.

Nick came in with Jay close at hand, of course, and they sat a few rows behind Farshad. It must be so annoying to have to deal with that little spaz all the time, Farshad thought to himself before realizing that Jay was actually holding on to Nick's arm. He was keeping Nick from teleporting.

That kid really didn't care how ridiculous he looked.

Farshad almost didn't notice Martina slip into the seat left of Nick. That seemed dangerous. If he was going to teleport, he'd probably teleport right into her. She didn't seem too worried. She also had four pencils and two pens, which she immediately used to draw in her sketchbook as if the second most important exam of the year wasn't about to take place. Farshad shook his head. He had to concentrate and this wasn't the time to be worrying about them.

"Oh, aren't you two just the cutest." Farshad heard Izaak's voice coming from behind him.

"Why thank you," Jay said, "I don't personally find you cute, but it is nice to hear."

"Shut up, faggot," Izaak snapped.

"You shut up," Nick growled.

Farshad turned around. Nick was standing up and everyone in the room was looking at him. He had turned beet red, but he kept standing as Izaak stared at him. "Oh look," Izaak said. "His boyfriend is going to defend him."

"Must I explain this to everyone?" Jay said, standing up and inserting himself between Nick and Izaak, "I feel like you're trying to insult us, but we don't think that being called homosexual is particularly insulting. Now, if I were to say something like 'You're a dimwitted Neanderthal' to you, it would be insulting. To Neanderthals." Jay smiled. "Because you're dumber than one."

Izaak grabbed Jay's shirt and yanked him over the table, shaking him like a rag doll, but quick as a snake Jay opened his mouth and clamped down on Izaak's hand with his teeth. "GAAAAAAHHH!" Izaak screamed, his voice surprisingly high-pitched.

"MR. CARPENTER!" Principal Jacobs bellowed, running up to them. Jay unlocked his jaw and Izaak clutched his hand, howling in pain.

"PRINCIPAL JACOBS!" Jay yelled back, otherwise completely composed.

"What on earth do you think you're doing?"

"HE BIT ME! THAT LITTLE FAGGOT FREAK BIT ME!" Izaak wailed.

"MR. MARCUS! I do not tolerate that sort of language in my school!"

"It really is intolerable," Jay said. "He also tastes disgusting."

"Mr. Carpenter, I suggest you stop talking. Take your things and go to Testing Room B immediately. Mr. Marcus, you're fine, stop howling like a great big squalling infant and sit down. I will deal with both of you after the exam is over. EVERYONE ELSE, there's nothing to see. Sit down and face front."

"But my dear Principal Jacobs, it is imperative that I remain—"

"Mr. Carpenter, NOW."

Farshad looked down at the table where his exam would soon be, determined to make himself as small and unnoticeable as possible. These were the people that were the closest thing he had to friends. It was infinitely better, he thought, not to have any friends at all.

AS SOON AS THE EXAM WAS OVER, COOKIE WAS out of her seat and heading for the door. She was pretty certain that she did well on the Fill In Your Name section of the test and also that she did miserably bad on the Everything Else section.

"Cookie, where are you going?" Addison asked as Cookie sped past the table where she was sitting with Claire and Emma.

"Gotta go, text you later," Cookie mumbled without looking back. As she left the cafeteria she could hear Emma blabbing on about the difficulty of the math section and how nervous she was to get the results back in two weeks. Ugh. Please. If you're good at something, don't pretend to be bad at it so that you look even better when oh my gosh, you did well. It irritated Cookie to no end.

"That wasn't fun," Martina said, falling in step next to Cookie.

"I swear, are you a cat or something? Maybe your super-special power is being a cat because you're crazy quiet and you just show up and I can never see you coming."

"I don't think so," Martina said. "Also, we have a cat and you can always see her coming, so I don't think you know much about cats."

"Cats are quiet and sneaky. You are quiet and sneaky. You are like a cat." They'd reached Cookie's locker. She opened it and started jamming her jacket into her messenger bag.

"Dinah is grossly overweight and not very sneaky. She falls down the stairs a lot. My sister thinks she looks like the poop emoji when she sits down." Martina leaned on the locker next to Cookie's. "Where are we going?"

"I don't know. Anywhere. Out of here. Away from Ms. Zelle."

"Would you like to go to Lancaster?" Martina asked.

"What? Lancaster? Why?"

"Abe wants to find his sister. He wants to find out what happened to her. Also I think he probably misses her."

"Why does he need us to go with him?"

"Probably because we're the only ones who won't judge him for what he's become."

Someone was approaching them. Nick. "I can't find Jay," he said.

"He's probably in Principal Jacobs's office," Martina said. "There's nothing you can do for him now. Are you ready to go?"

Cookie raised an eyebrow. "He's coming?"

"Of course."

"What about Farshad?"

Martina wrinkled her brow. "He was unreceptive."

"Surprise, surprise." Cookie looked down the hall at the crowds that had begun to file out of the cafeteria. It was only a matter of time before she was spotted with Nick and Martina. "Okay, fine. You two go, and I'll meet up with you."

"We'll be at the gym entrance parking lot," Martina said, and started to walk away.

"Wait, why aren't you coming with us right now?" Nick asked.

"Because she doesn't want to be seen with us," Martina said, looking at Cookie with strikingly light green eyes. It felt like she knew every terrible thought and feeling that Cookie had ever had. Hearing her own terrible thoughts and feelings spoken out loud hurt. And yet, as always, Martina didn't seem particularly bothered.

"I have to go the bathroom," Cookie said. "I'll meet you there."

Addison, Claire, and Emma were already in the bathroom when she got there. Of course.

"Hey, girl," Claire said, sidling up to Cookie. "Post-exam hangout?"

"Yeah, stranger," Addison said. "It's nice out. Let's walk into town."

"Maybe we could get some ice cream or something," Emma said, looking pointedly at Cookie.

"Yay! Ice cream! Come with us. Ice cream ice cream ice cream," Claire sang.

Just go with them, Cookie thought. *You can either just tune out the voices in your head and hang out with your friends—and their annoying little extra friend-person—or you can go with a bunch of weirdos on a mission to find out more about your own weirdness.* The choice seemed so clear—

Cookie couldn't have gone too far, she was just here.

I'll check by her locker.

"Sorry, rain check," Cookie said, giving Addison and Claire each an airy kiss on the cheek as she left the bathroom. She headed for the gymnasium exit. Once outside, she scanned the parking lot for Ed's car.

"You've got to be kidding me," she groaned when she saw the horse-drawn buggy. Nick and Martina were already in the back. She climbed in.

"Go go go," Cookie said to Abe through the front window. She turned to Martina and Nick. "I heard Ms. Zelle, she's looking for me again."

"Again?" Nick asked as the horse began to trot out of the parking lot.

"Yes. I heard her the other day." Cookie explained how she'd left Mrs. Whitaker's class after hearing Ms. Zelle's approach in her mind.

"All right," Nick said, "but you're saying this like she was doing something nefarious. Maybe she just wanted to talk to you about your grades."

"Okay, first, why are you assuming that my grades aren't good?"

Nick squirmed. "Maybe she wanted to . . . congratulate you for being such a good student?"

"That was a terrible save. Which brings me to my second point, which is why would she come get me during another teacher's class to either high-five me for being such a great student or to tell me that I'm a great big dumb-dumb? Teachers don't do that. They only pull you out of class if something tragic has happened, and even then the science teacher isn't going to be the one informing you that your dog died."

"I think it would have to be something bigger than that," Martina said, looking out the window. "It would probably have to be a human death. And it would still not be the science teacher." She turned to Cookie. "He just wants to trust Ms. Zelle because she's very pretty and he's attracted to her."

"HEY!" Nick blurted, blinking out and reappearing four inches to his left. Martina leaned over and put her hand on his knee. He looked equally furious and grateful for her assistance.

"Well, it's hard to believe, but sometimes even pretty people are untrustworthy," Cookie said with a roll of her eyes.

"I don't trust her," Abe called from the front of the cab. "Mostly because she entered my family's barn without permission and then tried to hurt me with a zapper and then set the barn on fire."

"Technically Mr. Friend set your barn on fire," Nick pointed out.

"Oh my god, listen to yourself." Cookie looked pointedly at Nick as he shifted awkwardly on the hard wood seat of Abe's buggy. "If nothing else, Ms. Zelle clearly can't be trusted." They were on a county road now and picking up speed. "Abe, could you tell Mr. Horse not to kill us all this time?"

"He did not kill us all last time," Abe said. "If he had done so, we would all be dead."

"Hey, Abe," Cookie said as the farmland flew by. "Do you even know where your sister lives?"

"No," the Amish boy said, "but someone told me where she works."

REBECCA LIVED ON THE TOP FLOOR OF A HOUSE ON the edge of town with a guy named Beanie, who was one of the other shunned Amish teenagers. They didn't seem to Nick to be boyfriend and girlfriend, although he would be the first to admit that he was never able to tell about these things anyway. They did have separate bedrooms.

The apartment was pretty bare. There was a small folding table near a kitchenette, two folding chairs, and a very ugly plaid sofa. Rebecca's bedroom door was closed but Nick could see what looked like a futon mattress on the floor of Beanie's room. Thinking about sleeping on it made Nick's back sore.

"Would anyone like anything to drink?" Rebecca asked after they'd all come in. Cookie asked for water and Rebecca seemed relieved that it was something she could actually provide (in a glass that read *Conestoga Valley Annual Beef & Beer Wrestling*). When she opened her fridge all Nick could see was some milk and what looked like a lot of packets of Nugget Town condiments.

Cookie and Nick sat on the plaid sofa and Martina sat cross-legged on the floor with her sketchbook in her lap. Abe remained standing. He looked unhappy and agitated.

"Do Daett and Maemm know that you're here?" Rebecca asked him.

"Neh," Abe said.

"Do they know where I am?"

"Ich vays nett." Abe began to twist his fingers into knots. "But I—we—need to talk to someone about something that you might know something about."

"All right," Rebecca said, sitting down on one of the folding chairs.

"It's about . . . the Hexerei."

Rebecca looked upset. "I am not . . . you need to know, I am not a Hexerei." Abe was silent. "Do you believe that I am a Hexerei?" she asked him, anguish in her voice.

"There have been strange things happening," Abe said, "and I don't know what to believe. But I believe that no matter what, you are my sister and you are a good person, and I will believe whatever you tell me." He looked at Nick, Cookie, and Martina.

"We'll believe you, too," Cookie said.

Rebecca looked at her with curiosity, and then back to Abe with a raised eyebrow. "We're all in this together," he told her, and began to tell the story of the past week. The storm. The bus accident. The invisible man who he thought was a ghost. Mr. Friend. Abe's ability to communicate with animals. Dr. Deery and the makeshift lab in Philadelphia. Occasionally he would lapse into Pennsylvania Dutch, but Nick could follow the thread. He already knew the story (although Abe's weaponizing of bird poop was news to him). Rebecca listened to it all, wide-eyed. "Wait," she said when he was finished, and went down the stairs.

She came back a minute later with a large, bored-looking gray cat. "Vemm sei grohi katz is sell?" Abe asked.

"My landlord's," Rebecca replied, setting the cat down on the bare wooden floor. "His name is Señor Fuzzybutt. Please," she said to Abe, gesturing to the cat.

Abe crouched down and looked into Señor Fuzzybutt's eyes. The cat lay down.

"There." Abe said.

Everyone was silent. "So . . . what are we looking at here?" Cookie asked.

"I made the cat lay down." Abe said.

Rebecca looked worried. "Are you sure?" She asked. "Señor Fuzzybutt lays down all the time. He might have just wanted to lay down." She looked at the cat, who had decided that it was the best possible moment to clean his own butt with his tongue. "Did you make him do that, too?"

"No!" Abe yelped. "He just wanted to be clean. Down there."

"Okay, Abe, can you make the cat do anything a little more interesting?" Cookie asked.

"I can't make animals do anything," he explained, "I ask

them politely to do something, and then if they feel like it they do it."

"So when you just asked the birds to poop all over the policeman?"

"Well . . . yes. They seemed happy to oblige. I think they enjoy pooping on people." Abe looked at the cat again.

Señor Fuzzybutt stopped licking himself, lay down again, and rolled over. Then he rolled over again. And again. And again until he hit the sofa.

"He's never done that before," Rebecca admitted.

"Rebecca," Cookie asked, "can you tell us what happened to make your family shun you?"

We were in Lancaster, living in a trailer that Sadie King's uncle lends to kids at Rumspringa.

It was Sadie, Jesse Hochstedler, Beanie, Willis Fisher, and me.

It was all so exciting at first—we'd never been on our own, or worn blue jeans, or been to a movie theater.

But we quickly discovered those things cost money. So we started to look for jobs.

Nugget Town is hiring.

That sounds greasy.

Most of us were feeling that we were going to return home eventually to commit ourselves to the Church, but we wanted to experience the outside world first.

She was offering a lot of money — enough for us to be able to go to any movie, buy any clothing we wanted — maybe even get a car.

They explained that we might get better at taking the tests, but none of us did.

I feel like we're failing you.

No, no!

You're doing great. I'll see you on Tuesday and we'll try again.

This went on for about a month. Every few days we'd be taken to the lab, given a few tests and some money.

Four more tests and we can get a car.

What are we going to do with a car when we go back home?

If it's this easy to make money I'm definitely not going back home.

When the scientists saw what Willis was writing they got very excited and asked if we wouldn't mind staying for some extra tests.

They brought us lunch and put us in a room with a few sofas and a mirror.

We've been here for hours. When are they going to bring Willis back?

At least we're getting paid to sit around.

But why is the door locked?

They probably just don't want us to wander around.

Right?

I don't know how long we were there—none of us had cell phones or watches or anything.

Days passed.

We ran. We ran and stayed out of sight. That first night we slept in an abandoned barn.

We made it home. We felt terrible, all decked out in English clothing and looking like something the cat dragged in. And we were really worried about Willis.

We have to go back. We have to find him.

But we don't know how to get back there.

And how would we get him back?

Let's tell the elders. They will be able to help us.

So we told Bishop Stolzfus. And then we showed him.

We scared him.

And that was when we were shunned.

No one would talk to us. We heard people whispering about us being Hexerei. It was unbearable, so we left. Beanie and I pooled our money and got this apartment.

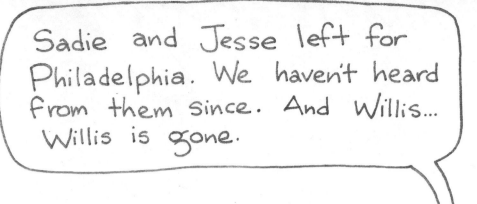

WHEN MARTINA HAD TOLD HIM THAT THEY WERE going to Lancaster, Farshad had done his best to gracefully bow out of the trip. "I can't, I'm busy," he'd told her.

Martina's eyes had turned a dark gray, and he'd wondered at the time how much longer it would be before someone else noticed. She never seemed particularly worried about it. "What are you doing?" she had asked.

Farshad blanked. His usual answer was "study" but they'd just finished the exam minutes before. "I . . . my parents need me. For stuff. For doing things. At home."

"It's all right if you don't want to go because it scares you," Martina had told him.

"I'm not scared."

"Okay."

"No, really, I'm not, I just don't think it's a good idea."

"All right."

"Do you think it's a good idea?" he'd asked her.

"It's an idea," she'd said, which didn't really answer his question in the slightest. "Would you like me to let you know what we find out?"

"Uh, sure," Farshad had said, even though he sort of didn't.

"Okay," she'd said, walking away.

"I'm not scared!" he'd found himself calling after her.

"Okay," she'd said, not turning around. She could be very unnerving, even when he wasn't seeing her eyes change colors every few minutes.

The rest of Farshad's weekend went by slowly. His parents drilled him on the test, asking what sort of questions were on it and how he thought he'd done. He thought he'd done well, particularly given the circumstances (the humming vending machines, the fear of breaking all his pencils with his freak thumbs, the sounds of Jay Carpenter's protests as he was led out of the cafeteria). But he omitted any mention of the drama and stuck to what he could remember of the exam. On Sunday he went for a long run, taking care not to find himself outside Cookie's house again.

Farshad was not happy to see Nick ambling up to him as he entered the school on Monday morning. "What's up?" Farshad asked him, trying to sound unfriendly without being too mean.

"Cookie wants you to meet up with us today after school," Nick started.

"Are you her errand boy now?" Farshad asked.

"No, we just thought that I'd probably be the best person to talk to you . . ."

"Farshad, old sport!" Jay came up behind him and clapped him on the back. "You will not believe the story that Nick and the others heard on Saturday. They tried to email you to meet up." He turned to Nick. "Did he get the email?" he asked. Nick looked at Farshad expectantly.

"I had some computer problems," Farshad said, and with a sigh of resignation, lowered his voice. "I accidentally smashed my dad's laptop with my thumbs."

"*Fantastic*," Jay breathed. "So you're meeting up with us at the Understeps after school, yes? Yes! Paul, old man!" Jay spotted Paul Yoder down the hall and bounded up to him.

"Is he friends with the Farm Kids?" Farshad asked Nick incredulously.

"They were in the other testing room when he was moved for the exam. They heard how he bit Izaak Marcus and now he's their hero." Nick looked grimly at his friend, who was chattering amiably with Paul and some of the other Farm Kids. "He has a way of forcing people to like him."

"That's insane. Why would he even want those guys to like him?"

"He doesn't care, actually. But they like him."

"I like him," Martina said, appearing next to Farshad as if from out of thin air. That girl was like a cat. "He's always interesting." She walked away.

"I am not used to her," Nick said.

"Truth," Farshad replied.

"But come to the meeting," Nick said. "I know you've got

your doubts, but you've got to hear what we found out." He lowered his voice. "It's about Auxano."

"Oh," Farshad said. "About that. Ms. Zelle called my parents and asked their permission for me to have my blood drawn when we go to Auxano with the Science Club field trip."

Nick's eyes widened. "You're kidding me."

"No. They're going to show us how to do differential centrifugation."

"That seems like a very terrible idea."

"It's just a process that separates organelles from whole cells . . ."

"I know what it is," Nick said, and thought a moment. "No, actually I don't, but that's not the point. It's a terrible idea for any of us to give our blood to Auxano. There's no way we can trust them with it."

"I'm still not convinced that Auxano is evil."

"Then tell me where Willis Fisher is."

"Who's Willis Fisher?"

'M COMING WITH YOU." JAY WAS RESOLUTE.

"I don't need anyone to come with me." Farshad was on the verge of turning around, leaving the Understeps, and never talking to the rest of them ever again. It was making Nick very nervous—it was hard enough enticing him to come to the meeting in the first place. Nick didn't think he had ever met anyone so guarded.

"Oh, on the contrary, my fine Persian American friend," Jay went on, "you need someone with you. Someone to have your back. A second set of eyes. A brother-in-arms. Someone that no one would ever suspect—"

"Jay, shut up." Cookie was agitated. "He shouldn't be going to Auxano in the first place." She turned to Farshad. "Just tell Ms. Zelle that you can't go. Tell her you don't feel well, or you're afraid of needles, or whatever. Just don't go."

"Why, because they're going to kidnap me and do experiments?"

"No, because once they realize that your blood is full of phlebotinum, their suspicions about the bus accident will be confirmed and then they're going to kidnap and do experiments on all of us!" Cookie said.

Farshad rolled his eyes. "Come on. Do you honestly think a company that employs half the people in this town—including *our parents*—would really kidnap anyone? Particularly us?"

"I don't know, why don't you tell me where Mr. Friend went? And where is Willis Fisher?"

Farshad threw his hands up in the air. "How should I know? I don't even know *who* Willis Fisher is. And neither do you. How could a teenager just disappear without anyone knowing about it? It doesn't make any sense."

"You see!" Jay chimed in. "You see, this is why I should come with you to Auxano. Your doubt is playing right into their diabolical hands—no offense to those amongst us—*ahem*—who have actual diabolical hands, specifically the thumb parts of their hands. I am far more savvy and can see what's really going on."

Martina let out a quick bark of a laugh without looking up from her sketchbook. Jay continued, unabated. "You are a scientist," he told Farshad.

"No, I'm not."

"You are in the Science Club, which is basically the same thing as being a scientist," Jay continued. "You believe what you see, and you haven't seen anyone kidnapping any poor Amish kids whose communities are so insular that they'd never report the disappearance anyway. Right?"

"Why are you even here?"

"Hush hush, I'm vital to this process." Jay bounded up to Farshad, who was easily a full head taller than he was. "You should go to Auxano, I will go with you, and we will be

SPIES. We will get to the bottom of what happened to Mr. Friend and Willis Fisher, and you will see for yourself that the company is not all that it seems."

"You're crazy," Cookie growled, turning to Nick. "Your freaky little friend is crazy."

"You're all crazy," Farshad said.

"I'm not," Martina said, eyes still locked on her drawing.

"Whatever. You're all crazy, it's been interesting knowing you, but as far as I'm concerned we're just some people who were in an accident with odd lingering side effects and there's really no reason that we have to keep meeting up. Stop trying to drag me into your crazy. I'm out." Farshad walked away.

Nick leaned back on the cool cinder-block wall and rubbed his temples. "He's going to tell them what happened. What we've become. This is bad. Very, very bad." He thought of Rebecca Zook in the bare little apartment, and how she lived in fear that Ms. Zelle was going to find her and take her away.

"Don't worry," Jay said, his mouth set in a firm line of determination. "I am going on that Science Club field trip, and if I have to take our Iranian friend down to keep him from talking, then that's what I'll do."

"And how exactly would you 'take him down'?" Cookie looked dubious.

"My dear lady, I believe I've proven myself more than capable of holding my own at physical combat. Ask Izaak Marcus, who now quakes with fear at the mere mention of my name."

"Jay, please don't bite Farshad," Nick pleaded.

"Biting would be a last resort. I care too much about my overall dental health to go around biting people willy-nilly," Jay promised. "I'm going to go on that trip and I'm going to make sure that Farshad doesn't do anything that would put the rest of you at risk, because I care very deeply for each of you."

"Thank you, Jay." Martina said.

"You're welcome, Martina, you beautiful and insightful goddess."

"This is ridiculous," Cookie said. "How would you even go on the field trip? Are you even in the Science Club?"

Jay laughed.

"What?" Cookie asked.

Nick looked at Cookie. "You have to understand," he explained. "This is Jay. Inserting himself into situations where he doesn't belong is what he does best."

"Damned straight, old boy."

COOKIE CHECKED HER PHONE AS SHE WALKED home. It had been oddly quiet since the exam, so she shut it down and then restarted it. Still nothing. No texts. She shot one off to Addison and Claire, asking where they were. No response. That was irritating.

Maybe she had texted too much and her mom had shut off her account? No, that couldn't be it, they had unlimited texting. Maybe there was just something wrong with the system. Maybe someone totally random had been affected by phlebotinum and now had the ability to block wireless communications.

Her phone buzzed, and Cookie tried to look nonchalant as she checked to see who it was from (even though no one was watching her, but you never knew). It was a text from her mom, asking if she was coming home for dinner or eating at Claire's house. Cookie texted back that she was on her way home, and her mom replied with a happy-faced emoji. Her phone was working. Whatever magical, unknowable power that allowed her thumb-typed messages to fly through the ether and end up on her mother's phone was working.

Were Addison and Claire seriously not answering her texts?

That was ridiculous. Maybe there was something wrong with their phones. Yes, that made sense. Cookie could see it—they'd probably been in the bathroom together, looking at their phones at pictures of their celebrity crushes or kittens or whatever and then Addison went to show Claire what was on her phone just as Claire went to show Addison what was on her phone and they knocked heads and the phones flew out of their hands and landed in the toilet and then they had to go home and dismantle the phones and put the pieces in a bowl of dried rice and once their phones were working again they'd text Cookie and they'd all laugh together.

Wait, that didn't seem right. The being in the bathroom and showing each other their phones part made sense, but why would they be doing that over an open toilet? That made no sense.

Maybe they'd been kidnapped.

Maybe Ms. Zelle had a team of Auxano enforcers that were roaming the streets, picking up middle school girls, and taking them back to the secret lab to test their blood.

Probably not.

But maybe she should go by Claire's house anyway, just to make sure that everything was okay. It was sort of on her way home.

Fifteen minutes later Cookie was standing outside Claire's house. She'd been there a million times—Claire's mom had told her more times than she could count that Cookie was welcome there whenever she wanted. She was practically part of the family. She had never before hesitated to march up to the front door and walk right in. But now . . .

You have to make them believe that she was at the ice cream parlor.

You have to tell them about it, but don't be intense about it. Make her sound like the crazy one. They're already annoyed with her. This is the perfect time.

Come on, you can do this. This is your chance to take down Cookie Parker.

Emma Lee's thoughts settled directly into Cookie's brain. She was inside Claire's house with Claire and Addison, and she was about to tell them about Cookie's weird ice cream date with Farshad Rajavi and a girl who drew pictures of herself with alien antennae. Cookie was aghast.

NO. Her brain screamed at Emma Lee, *YOU WILL SHUT UP. YOU WILL SHUT UP AND BE SHUTTING UP AND STAY SHUT UP.*

Cookie felt the tears prickling in the corners of her eyes. She had been considering just walking into Claire's house and making herself at home as if Claire had actually answered her text, but now there was no way—if Addison and Claire saw her tears she'd look like the biggest loser ever. Never let them see that they've upset you. She backed away from Claire's house, and as soon as she was absolutely certain that no one could see her, Cookie started to cry.

IT WAS BAD ENOUGH THAT JAY CARPENTER HAD SOMEHOW managed to invite himself along for the Science Club trip to Auxano; that he insisted on being in Ms. Zelle's car with Farshad made it all so much worse. Not that Farshad wanted to be alone in the car with a woman he didn't trust, but he really didn't want to be in a car with that woman and Jay. He was probably the most annoying person Farshad had ever met.

"So," Jay said, straining against the child-safe backseat safety belt to lean forward as much as possible. "What are we going to see? Are we going to see a centrifuge? I have always wanted to see an industrial-sized centrifuge."

"Actually, we are," Ms. Zelle said. "I didn't know you were so interested in science, Jay."

"But of course I am!" Jay said. "I'm terribly interested in science. I'm actually interested in everything. I'd go so far as to say I'm a polymath. Did you know that ancient Sumerians believed that after you died you went to a world made of clay where there was nothing but clay as far as the eye could see and nothing to eat except for more clay?"

"I did not know that," Ms. Zelle admitted.

"Archaeology is just one of my many interests. Just like zoology. Did you know that wombats poop cubes?" Jay asked, and continued talking before Ms. Zelle could answer. "Are we going to be able to use the centrifuge? Can I touch the centrifuge?"

Ms. Zelle laughed. "No, but we will be seeing it used."

"What are we going to be putting in the centrifuge?"

"Farshad's blood, actually." Ms. Zelle quickly looked over at Farshad and smiled. "He's volunteered to be our guinea pig today. Are you nervous?" she asked him.

"No," Farshad said, lying.

"Why Farshad's blood?" Jay asked. Farshad felt a cold chill run up his back.

"Oh, because we thought it would be fun if it came from one of the club members." Ms. Zelle said lightly.

"That does sound fun," Jay said. "Can I do it? Can it be my blood?"

"Sorry, Jay, it has to be Farshad's. His parents already signed the permission form."

"Tragic. I feel like I'm missing out on the fun," Jay said.

"Don't worry, you'll get to see the whole process."

The rest of the Science Club (two other boys and one girl named Kitty, who Farshad had always considered his main rival for valedictorian) were in a car with the other science teacher, Mr. Greene, a quiet man who always looked terrified of his own students. Ms. Zelle parked next to his car and the two groups merged to walk into the main lobby of the Auxano headquarters.

Farshad was familiar enough with the building. He had been there countless times with his parents and on field trips, but as he entered the main lobby he felt his stomach drop with a fear that he'd never before felt. Without thinking about it he balled his hands into fists, wrapping this thumbs in his other fingers.

"Don't worry, old boy," Jay said in an uncharacteristically low voice, "I've got your back."

Farshad said nothing but gave him a slight, almost imperceptible nod.

"Okay everybody!" Ms. Zelle said, "Gather round, gather round. Who's ready to see the new ultracentrifuge?"

"YEAH!" Jay yelled, pumping his fist in the air.

"Yes!" Kitty added, temporarily caught up in Jay's enthusiasm. He winked at her and she immediately turned beet-red.

"Follow me!" Ms. Zelle said, and they headed to an elevator that would bring them to a lower-level lab, stopping at a row of lab coats hanging on the wall and handing them out to everyone. "Most of the labs are underground." Ms. Zelle said, "Can anyone tell me why?"

Kitty's hand shot up.

"Kitty, we're not in the classroom, you can just call out an answer if you know it." Ms. Zelle explained. Kitty turned red again.

"Because the temperature is more stabilized when there's no chance of natural sunlight?" Kitty asked.

"Exactly," Ms. Zelle said, "ten points to Gryffindor. It's also where Auxano keeps dungeons full of huuuuuuumans to experiment on." Farshad paled while the rest of the group chuckled.

"Ooh, can we go to the dungeons? Is that where Auxano stores the mutants?" Jay asked.

"You are too much, Jay." Ms. Zelle laughed, shepherding them into the elevator.

Jay's head darted around as Ms. Zelle ushered them into the lab. He appeared to be scanning the large room for electronic access panels to secret chambers.

"Ms. Zelle was joking about the dungeon, you moron," Farshad growled at the little freak.

"Poppycock."

"Are you serious? Did you seriously just say *poppycock*?"

"I did indeed and I'll do it again. Poppycock. One of the best ways to hide is to do so in plain sight; if you're trying to hide something utterly outlandish, tell anyone and everyone. Everyone will think it's a great big joke and no one will believe for a second that it's true. For instance, if you had just laughed and told everyone that you were a terrorist then no one would have believed you and your reputation would have been sterling."

"But that doesn't make any sense, because I'm not actually a terrorist."

"Ah, right. Bad example. A good example would be our dearest deadly Ms. Zelle telling everyone that there are dungeons full of chemically altered humans like Willis Fisher and Mr. Friend. No one believes her but we know that she's actually telling the truth."

"You believe that she's telling the truth. I believe that you're a nutball."

"Look at us, the believer and the skeptic. We are going to make a great team." Jay punched Farshad lightly on the arm. Farshad glowered at him. It had no effect whatsoever.

"Okay, okay, everyone, gather round," Ms. Zelle called. "Farshad, you sit here and roll up your sleeve." Farshad sat in a wide chair next to her while a lab technician with a thick mustache prepped a needle. He spied Mr. Greene standing in the corner as far away from the tech as possible. The science teacher wasn't looking too hot.

"Roll up your sleeve, please," the tech asked, and quickly tied a rubber tourniquet around Farshad's arm. He placed a squishy stress toy shaped like a brain in Farshad's hand. "Can you squeeze this a few times?"

Farshad squeezed the brain, taking care not to use his thumb. Is this what it was going to be like for the rest of his life? Always having to be hyperaware of his thumbs? The tech advanced with the needle, and behind him Farshad could see Jay. He looked worried. Farshad looked down and felt the sharp pinch as the needle slid into his arm. A vial attached to the syringe by a rubber tube quickly filled with his blood.

Farshad heard a loud crash and looked up. Mr. Greene had fainted dead away. Ms. Zelle rushed to kneel by his prone body. "Did anyone see if he hit his head?" she asked.

The tech with the mustache took the needle out of Farshad's arm and gave him a folded wad of gauze to press against it. "Keep your arm elevated for a minute," Mustache said. "I'll be back with a Band-Aid in a second." Farshad watched as the tech slipped the vial of his blood into another tech's hand. The other tech quickly and quietly left the room. Farshad shot a look to Jay. Jay nodded, and slipped out the door after the tech with the blood.

Farshad began to panic. He thought he had given Jay a look that had clearly meant, *Hey, look, they're taking my blood away*, not, *GO FOLLOW MY BLOOD!* What was that little weirdo going to do? Would he bite the lab tech?

Mr. Greene groaned and tried to sit up. "Steady, steady," Ms. Zelle said. The lab tech with the mustache came back to Farshad and put a Band-Aid over the square of gauze.

"I'm fine, I'm fine. I just have a thing about blood. This is so embarrassing," Mr. Greene muttered.

"Do you need anything?" Ms. Zelle asked him as he got up.

"I think I saw a vending machine in the hall," Farshad volunteered. "I can get him a drink or something."

Ms. Zelle reached into her purse and gave Farshad two dollars. "Come back quick, we're going to put your blood into the ultracentrifuge as soon as Mr. Greene is better."

"I'm better."

Ms. Zelle rolled her eyes. "Go go go, get him some orange juice if they have any."

Farshad headed out the door into the hall, and kept walking past the vending machine, desperately wishing that he had Cookie's ability to hear people's thoughts about directions. He turned one corner, and then another, and started testing doors.

Locked. Locked. Locked. Locked. Supply closet. Locked. This was ridiculous. How was he supposed to find Jay? Ms. Zelle was going to start looking for him any second. Bathroom, locked. Farshad gingerly opened a door marked Security.

There was no one inside. Farshad looked at a bank of small television screens showing different areas of the building. The lobby, labs, lots of nondescript hallways, a room with a man strapped to a bed by his wrists and ankles, employee break room . . .

MR. FRIEND.

Farshad gaped at the television screen. There he was: Mr. Friend. Farshad quickly scanned the rest of the screens. Different angle of the lobby. Back entrance. Room full of rabbit cages. A teenage boy pacing a room with a cot in it, writing on a wall with a pencil. Farshad could see writing on all the walls. Mathematical equations?

"Can I help you?" Farshad spun around to see an Auxano security guard. The locked bathroom . . .

"I . . ." Farshad was at a loss for words. The security guard leapt forward and grabbed Farshad, deftly pinning his arms behind his back and pushing him up against a filing cabinet. Farshad cried out in pain.

"WHO ARE YOU? WHAT ARE YOU DOING HERE?" the security guard bellowed into Farshad's ear. He was huge and his breath smelled like onions. Farshad was terrified.

"My name is Farshad Rajavi! I'm here on a field trip with my science class! I got lost! Oww!"

"A likely story," the security guard said, pushing Farshad against the filing cabinet. The handles of the drawers dug into Farshad's rib cage.

"I swear it's true I go to Deborah Read Middle School my teacher is Ms. Zelle my mom works here just ask for Miryam Rajavi she works here find my mom . . ."

"Farshad, old boy, what on earth are you doing here?" Jay strode into the room and seemed completely undisturbed by the fact that a two-hundred-pound gorilla dressed as a security guard was slowly crushing Farshad. "Ms. Zelle was about to call security to find you and here you are, already with security! And you're hugging. That's nice. Lab time! We're going to do experiments, huzzah!" Jay walked up to the security guard, who looked very confused but had not let go of Farshad.

"And hello to you!" Jay said excitedly. "I'm Jay Carpenter, and I'm a polymath. Do you know what a polymath is? Of course you do, I can see that you're a man of great wit, why else would you choose to work around geniuses all day? Marvelous! I have a song about being a polymath that I've been working on, would you like to hear it?"

"No," the security guard said, bewildered. He had loosened his grip on Farshad's arm.

"Of course you would! *I am a polymath. I'm very clean because I like a hot bath . . .*"

"Where are you boys supposed to be?" the guard asked, looking at Farshad for the first time as though he might actually be just a lost kid.

"Wait, wait, I'm about to get to the good part," Jay continued, singing, *"I like so many things, like car parts and bottles and cutlery and whatever I find lying around . . ."*

"Enough," the security guard growled. "Do you know how to get back to your group?"

"Of course we do! And you're right, we should go, Ms. Zelle will be worried. Ta-ta, Officer!" Jay grabbed Farshad's arm and steered him out of the security office. "Are you all right?" he asked as soon as they were out of earshot.

"No. Yes. No. I'm fine," Farshad said, feeling the pain in his arm and his rib cage. He was eager to put as much distance between himself and the room as possible. "Were you able to get the blood?" he asked Jay in a low voice.

"Unfortunately no," Jay said, guiding him back to the hallway where the vending machine was. "But I saw where they put it."

"We have to get it back," Farshad said. "We have to. Cookie was right about everything."

"She is magical, isn't she?"

So – you guys are a study group?
Yeah.
Wasn't the exam a few days ago?
We're getting a head start on the next one.
Wow.
Hello there.
Good day.
Okay. This was fun. Gotta pee.

NICK TRIED TO BREATHE. IN THROUGH THE NOSE, OUT through the mouth, remaining calm, not going anywhere. Martina had her hand on his arm, so he knew he wasn't going anywhere, but he didn't want to spend the rest of his life tethered to her. Not that he minded her hand on his arm. It wasn't like she had a clammy hand or anything, but, knowing Martina, she probably wanted to use it to draw in her sketchbook.

She'd put her hand on his arm when Farshad and Jay were telling their story. Jay did most of the talking, of course, and at first it sounded like another one of Jay's crazy tall tales, like the time he'd told Nick and his mom that he'd done some genealogical research and was pretty sure that he was a direct descendent of Benjamin Franklin. But Farshad was backing up everything that Jay was saying, and Nick began to feel incredibly nervous. They had Farshad's blood, which meant they would soon figure out that he was . . . odd, and then it was only a matter of time before they realized that they were all odd. And then they'd end up locked up like Mr. Friend and Willis Fisher.

"The last time I saw Farshad's blood, it was in a fridge in a lab near the security room. That was four hours ago," Jay said.

"Do you think you could draw a map?" Ed asked. Nick jumped a little. Having the invisible man around was unnerving.

"Why, what's the plan?" Jay asked.

"I'm going to go and get the blood." Ed said. "That's the plan."

"Yes!" Jay said, forcefully slamming his hand down on the breakfast buffet. "We need to strategize. Ed is our guy for stealth, clearly, and Farshad is the muscle. Daniesha, we'll need you to hone your skills . . ."

"What?" Ed said, clearly startled. "No. *I* am going to go and get the blood. No one else is coming with me. That is the plan. I'm going tonight. Abe, you can come with me as far as the campus. I'll need you to get into the driver's seat so that nothing looks suspicious. The rest of you—and yes, I'm looking at all of you right now and pointing my finger at you . . ."

"He is," Martina confirmed.

"The rest of you have to stay put. I'm done having you play spy—I appreciate what you've learned, but it's time for me to take over. I'll find the blood."

"We can't just sit here," Farshad said, clearly frustrated. "It's my blood. It's my fault that it's there. I need to get it back."

"I'm going to get it back," Ed said. "You've done enough."

"I should go," Cookie said.

"No, you really shouldn't," Ed snapped.

"And how will you explain Abe sitting alone in a car

outside of the Auxano campus?" Cookie asked. "An Amish weirdo, alone in a car, doing nothing? If I'm with him then we can at least tell people we were on a date or something."

Abe immediately turned so red that Nick was momentarily worried that his head would actually explode. "I . . . I don't think . . ." the Amish boy stuttered.

"Plus Abe is terrible under pressure," Cookie interrupted. "If I'm there I can keep him from saying the wrong thing. Or anything."

"But . . . but . . . it would not look realistic for us to be romantically involved," Abe stammered.

"I'll wear a little lipstick, it will make me look old enough," Cookie said dismissively.

"I cannot date a black girl!" Abe blurted.

The room fell silent as Cookie gave the trembling Amish teenager a hard stare. After a moment, Jay stood up.

"It's decided then. I will go instead of Abe."

"How are you going to convince anyone that you're old enough to drive?" Farshad asked. "You're the size of a peanut."

"One small peanut can take down an army, my friend, providing that everyone in the army has a severe peanut allergy . . ."

"Enough!" Ed's disembodied voice rang throughout the kitchen. "That's enough. Abe is coming with me. Cookie, you are also coming with us, and you're not going to kill Abe, he's not used to people like you."

"People like me. REALLY?"

"Yes, really. Black people. Look at him. He looks like he's going to pass out."

Cookie looked at Abe. "Maybe Jay should be the one to come with me."

"YES!"

"No," Ed said, "like it or not, Abe is the only one who looks old enough to drive a car. And Cookie is the only one who seems to be able to keep it together under pressure."

"Hey!" Nick said, hurt.

"I'm sorry, but you're going to transport yourself into a wall and Farshad's the one who thought it was a good idea to give Auxano a blood sample in the first place despite everything my brother told you." There was a silence as everyone in the room turned to Martina.

"And none of you know what to make of me," she said.

Ed snapped his fingers. The sudden noise made Nick jump a little. "Abe, Cookie, let's go," he said. "The rest of you? STAY. HERE."

Abe stood miserably as Cookie got up and put on her jacket. She looked grim. "Be careful," Nick told her.

"I will," she said.

"And try not to kill Abe," Martina advised.

"I'm not making any promises."

"Daniesha," Jay said, inserting himself directly in front of her and snatching her phone.

"Hey!" Cookie tried to grab the phone back but Jay quickly ducked behind the breakfast bar while he typed furiously into her phone.

"I'm inputting my emergency cell phone number. If you are in trouble and need us, text to ask about how the kittens are doing. If you're fine, email to ask how the puppies are doing."

Cookie leaned over the bar and yanked the phone out of his hands. "Why would I email you if everything is fine?" she asked.

"To chat. If you wanted to chat."

"UGH." Cookie turned on her heel and followed Abe out the door to Ed's car. Nick, Jay, Martina, and Farshad watched as it drove away with her in the backseat and Abe sitting shotgun.

"Okay," Jay said as the car disappeared around a corner. "Let's get moving."

"Let's get moving where?" Farshad asked.

"To Auxano, of course." Jay said. "They're going to need us and it's a long walk, so we might as well get started."

Farshad picked up his backpack. "Right. But we're stopping by my house first to get a change of clothing and my mom's work access card."

"Good man."

Nick stared at them in astonishment. Had everyone completely lost their minds?

Martina packed her sketchbook into her bag and looked at him with big dark green eyes. "You coming?"

ABE SAT IN THE FRONT SEAT OF ED'S CAR WITH HIS hands gripping the steering wheel. They were parked on the side of the road near the woods that bordered the Auxano campus. Cookie had moved into the front seat and was amusing herself by staring at the clearly terrified Abe.

"So," she said after a while. "How are you doing?"

Abe said nothing.

"Anything new going on in your world?" They could see the top of Auxano's main building over the tree line. There wasn't much else to look at, besides each other, and Abe seemed determined to avoid even a quick glance in Cookie's direction.

"So," she continued, "on a scale of Uncomfortable to Completely Freaked Out, would you say that you're nervous around me or crazy scared?"

Abe gripped the steering wheel a little tighter.

"Whatever," Cookie said, fishing her phone out of her bag. Maybe she should email "puppies" to Jay just to make his day. The kid was weird and super annoying, but at least being around her didn't make him go into a catatonic state.

Abe shifted uncomfortably. "I am not scared of you," he said carefully. Cookie looked up from her phone. "But I do not want you to have the wrong idea about what we are doing here."

Cookie raised an eyebrow. "And what do you think that I think we're doing here exactly?"

"Well . . ." Abe looked incredibly uncomfortable. "It is important that you know . . ."

"Mmmmmyes?"

"It is important that you know that we're not actually on a date."

Cookie stared at him.

"I am not interested in you in that way and we are just pretending to be on a date if someone wonders what we are doing here. And if they do, we will not be kissing or hugging. We will just tell them that we are on a date." He turned to her, looking pleased with himself for getting it all out. "Do you understand?"

"So what you're saying is that if anyone should come by for any reason, we should immediately start making out like crazy bunnies."

Abe looked incredibly confused. "No, no, I do not think you understand what I am trying to tell you . . ."

"No, I totally get it. If we even think that someone might be driving by us, I should immediately jump on you and we should smush our mouths together."

"That is the opposite of what we should do!" He looked terrified.

Cookie smiled. She knew that torturing a dumb Amish

kid wasn't a particularly kind thing to do, even if he was clearly pretty racist. She couldn't even be angry about that—she was probably the first black person he'd ever spoken to, and now he was trapped alone with her in a parked car. But that didn't mean that she couldn't mess with him a little. Or a lot.

"So let me get this straight," she said, "if a person were to come by and say, 'Hey, what are you kids doing?' we should just yell, 'WE'RE IN LOVE!' and then you'll immediately get down on one knee and ask me to marry you, and we'll lick each others' faces. That's the plan, right?"

"No! No! That is not a good plan! I could never marry you! We are never getting married!!!" Abe looked like he was about to have a heart attack.

"Oh my god, dude. CHILL. Don't worry. I'm not going to touch you with my scary black face." Cookie looked back down at her phone. "You need to calm down. I don't want you accidentally using your power to summon a nearby bear to eat us or something."

"Bears do not eat people under normal circumstances. And also, rabbits do not kiss each other." Abe took his hands off the steering wheel to rub his temples. "Where is Mr. Ed? Can you hear him?"

"A little," Cookie said. She'd been hearing him navigate the hallways of Auxano for a while, along with about ten or so other faint voices in her head of other people. One woman was trying to find the entrance to the highway— another couldn't find a bathroom. She was getting a little better at tuning them out in order to focus on Ed's thoughts. "He's trying to find an empty stairwell so that he doesn't have to use the elevator."

Abe perked up. "I have been in an elevator," he said, almost as if he was telling her an exciting secret.

"No. Really? What was it like?"

"It was incredible," he said. This kid wouldn't know sarcasm if it came up to him in the middle of an empty field in broad daylight and said, *Hello, Abe, I'm Sarcasm!* "I knew that I was being pulled up, but it was almost as if I had stepped into a magical box that transported me to an entirely different place."

"Wow."

"It was really something."

"Sounds like it was." Cookie leaned back and closed her eyes.

Down the stairs. To the left. Past the vending machine.

"He's almost there," she told Abe.

"So you hear him? Do you hear words?"

"Yeah. It's kind of like when you're talking to yourself in your head, only someone else is doing the talking, and they're not talking to you."

"But you cannot hear what I am thinking right now." Abe looked worried.

"You're thinking, 'Scary black girl is scaring me.'"

Abe's eyes widened. "I was not thinking that! I might have been feeling that, but I was not using those words in my head!"

"Oh my god, Abe, calm down. You're going to rip the steering wheel off of its column. I'm messing with you. Unless you're thinking about directions, or telling yourself what you want to do, I can't hear you."

"Then how did you know what I was feeling?"

"Are you serious?"

Abe nodded.

"I can tell what you're feeling because I'm clearly the first black person that you've ever interacted with. When you work up the nerve to actually look at me it's like you're looking at a scary animal. Like I'm a tiger or something. It's pretty clear what you're feeling towards me." Cookie looked back down at her phone.

They sat in silence. "You know," Abe said after a moment, "if I get shunned I am going to have to get used to a lot of different sorts of people." He relaxed his grip on the steering wheel. "Maybe it is good that you are black so that I can get used to people like you."

"Yes," Cookie said. "Thank goodness I'm here to gently introduce you to the exotic ways of my people."

"Exactly!"

"Oh my god, shut up."

"Why? What did I say?"

COOKIE!

In her mind Cookie could hear Ed calling out to her. He was deliberately thinking about how to get out of the room he was in, to go down the hallway, up the stairs, out the back delivery entrance and through the field up to the car . . .

CAN'T GET OUT. TRAPPED HERE.

"Something's wrong." Cookie whispered.

"What did I say?"

"You were being a dumb racist, but that's not the problem right now. Ed's trapped in the building. They've got him."

Abe's eyes widened. "We need to tell the others about kittens!"

"What's that I heard about kittens?" Jay asked, popping his head into Cookie's open window.

"GAAAH!"

"Hello gorgeous."

NICK TWISTED AROUND AND TELEPORTED A FEW times to see if anyone had heard Cookie's scream. She looked furiously at Jay, who was just happy to have her attention. Cookie quickly opened the door, knocking Jay aside before getting out of the car. "Oops," she muttered as Nick helped him up.

"What were you saying about kittens?" Nick asked.

"They've got Ed. They somehow detected that he was there and now they have him." Cookie said. "I think he's trying to tell me that he wants us to go back to Philly to get Dr. Deery."

"And what's Dr. Deery supposed to do?" Farshad asked.

"Save him?" Martina asked.

"Rubbish," Jay said, pulling dried leaves out of his hair. "He'd get caught as soon as he tried to get into the building."

"And then we'd never get Dr. Deery's cure," Cookie said.

"Hmmph. I'm not so certain that a cure is what you all need, but we'll address that issue at a later date," Jay said. "We've got to get into that building, get the blood, and save Ed." Jay looked at Abe. "And we're going to get your Amish friend."

Nick gawked at his friend. He was used to Jay telling him what to do, but it was very different to watch him take charge of other people. People who might not realize how deeply wacky Jay's plans usually were. "Sounds great," he said to Jay. "And exactly how are we going to do that?"

Jay turned around and grabbed Nick.

"MY GOD, MAN," he yelled, "how many times do we have to go over this?" Jay looked around at the group. "YOU. HAVE. SUPERPOWERS."

"WE. HAVE. OKAYISH POWERS," Nick shot back, frustrated. "And we're kids. We're not super spies. We could also get caught and then what? End up trapped like Ed? Like Mr. Friend? Like the Amish kid?"

"We're going to end up caught if we don't go in there and get the blood," Cookie said quietly. "They're going to figure out that Farshad has been exposed to phlebotinum and then they're coming after the rest of us. Ms. Zelle already suspects that something is up with me. We can't let them have any proof." She looked over at Farshad, who had taken off his jeans. "What are you doing???"

"Nice undies," Martina observed.

"Okay, kindly look away while I put on clothing that makes me look like an adult." Farshad quickly grabbed a pair of khakis out of his bag while Nick moved to shield him with his body. "You couldn't have done this in your house?" Nick asked.

"I didn't want them to get all messed up on the walk over," Farshad said, pulling a leather belt through the loops in his pants. "Here," he said to Abe, throwing him a buttoned long-sleeved shirt, "change into this."

"I can't wear this," Abe said, aghast.

"Well, you can't wear that," Cookie said, eyeing his short-sleeved shirt and black suspenders. "You look Amish."

"I am Amish!"

"Amish people don't work in scientific laboratories, you dink."

"It has buttons!"

"I can help you figure out the buttons."

Abe turned so red Cookie began to believe that he would actually pass out from embarrassment. Jay gently pushed her aside and grabbed Abe's arm. "Allow me," he said, leading Abe into the woods near the car.

"This is crazy." Nick fretted. "Do we even have a plan?"

"Yes." Martina said. "Nick, you will use your power to get in the same back door that Ed went through and then let me, Cookie, and Jay in. Farshad and Abe will use Dr. Rajavi's access card to go through the front door and pick up lab coats for us so that if security sees us on their cameras we'll just look like anyone working in a lab. We'll meet up with them to get our coats and split into three teams; Farshad and Abe, Jay with you, and me with Cookie, because Jay, Cookie, and Farshad know their way around the best."

Nick stared at Martina. This was the most he'd ever heard her talk and it was freaking him out a little.

"Nick and Jay will look for the vials of blood," Martina continued. "Farshad and Abe will look for Willis Fisher. And Cookie and I will look for Ed, because I'm the only one who can see him. Once we have the blood, Ed, and Willis, we can head back out through the back door and go our separate ways. We can meet up here." Martina looked back down at her sketchbook as if she hadn't just spoken ALL THE WORDS.

Nick, Cookie, and Farshad looked at each other, and then to Jay and Abe, who had emerged from the woods. Abe still looked like a teenager, but in a normal shirt and without his hat Nick figured that he might be able to pass for a college kid. Farshad was less hunched over. He was at least six feet tall and looked a lot older.

"Sounds like a plan to me," Farshad said.

"Wait," Cookie said, walking up to Abe. She reached up to touch him and he immediately recoiled. "Stay still," she commanded, and tousled his hair so that he looked less like an enormous toddler. "Look, I didn't kill you. I touched you and you didn't die. Although," she said, taking a step back and surveying her work, "you still might. Breathe already."

Nick looked at the rest of the group. Cookie looked like she was trying not to look worried. Farshad looked determined. Jay was nearly shaking with excitement, and Martina looked . . . Martina looked like she always looked, as if throwing one's self into the deep end of the crazy pool was a perfectly pleasant way to spend an evening.

"Let's do this," Cookie said. "Let's get some blood."

SOMETHING ABOUT THE WAY THAT MARTINA HAD spoken (or maybe the mere fact that she had spoken more than two sentences in a row) had made Farshad feel like the plan was really solid, but as they approached the imposing front doors of Auxano's main building he began to feel less confident. Farshad knew that being tall and brown made him seem older, but having Abe silently freaking out next to him wasn't helping to maintain that illusion.

"Just do what I do, okay?" Farshad said before they entered the lobby. "You just have to act confident, like you belong here." Farshad wondered if he could channel his inner Cookie.

"But we don't belong here," Abe said. He looked incredibly uncomfortable in Farshad's button-down shirt. "What if they start asking questions?"

"I'll do all the talking," Farshad said.

"And what if they talk to me?" Abe implored.

"I don't know, pretend you don't speak English," Farshad said, pushing open the lobby doors.

When Farshad had come in with the field trip, Ms. Zelle had given the front desk receptionist a quick wave and then taken the group straight past her to where the lab coats and elevators were. *Project assuredness*, Farshad thought, walking confidently past the front desk. *Act like you own the place. Act like Cookie Parker.*

"Excuse me?" the front desk receptionist asked. Farshad stopped walking and turned around. He tried to smile without looking creepy.

"Yes?" he asked. "I'm sorry, I can't talk long, we're in a hurry."

"You haven't swiped your ID card," the receptionist explained, eyeing them suspiciously.

"Oh," Farshad said, "of course." He dug his mother's card out of his pocket and waved it at a small plastic black panel near the receptionist. Behind her he could see his mother's ID photo pop up on the computer screen. *DON'T TURN AROUND!* his brain screamed to the woman, but she was looking at Abe, who was looking around at the modern lobby in complete wonder.

"Dr. Tam," he said, using the fake name that Jay had assigned Abe. Farshad had thought it was silly at the time, but now he was grateful that he wasn't using their actual names. Unfortunately, Abe seemed oblivious. "Dr. Tam," Farshad growled. Abe looked at him, startled.

"You'll have to excuse my colleague, he's just in from overseas and he's a little jet-lagged," Farshad explained to the receptionist.

"Do you need a visitor's pass?" the receptionist asked Abe.

"Ich habb dich nett fashtanna," he said.

"I'm sorry, his English is a little rough," Farshad said. "A visitor's pass would be great."

The receptionist nodded and handed Abe a neon sticker with the date stamped on it. Abe looked mystified as to what he was supposed to do with it. Farshad peeled the sticker off of its backing and slapped it on Abe's chest. "Danki!" Abe said. The receptionist looked at him with undisguised curiosity. Abe smiled and waved at her.

"Okay, time to go now, they're waiting for us," Farshad said, steering Abe toward the hallway with the lab coats.

"How did I do?" Abe asked when they were out of earshot.

"Fine, but you've got to stop looking like you've never seen a corporate lobby before."

"But I haven't. It's so big and there's so much light. Have you ever been to the Taj Mahal?"

"You know I'm not Indian, right?"

"Really? What are you?" Abe asked.

"I'm American," Farshad said.

They put on lab coats, gathered four more, and headed to the elevator. "Can I press the button?" Abe asked.

"Knock yourself out." Abe looked inordinately pleased as he pressed the button and it lit up. "Abe. Seriously. Be cool." Farshad said. Abe did his best to compose his face.

"You think I act like I own the place?" Cookie asked as soon as the elevator doors opened. She was standing in the hall with her hands on her hips next to Nick, Jay, and Martina. She was clearly annoyed.

"You heard that?" Farshad gaped. "I wasn't thinking about directions!"

"You were directing yourself to do something, so I guess I heard you."

"Guys," Nick said in a low voice as he took one of the lab coats from Abe and put it on. "Now is not the time. If we somehow get out of this, then you can all be mad at each other."

"Oh, I'm not mad," Cookie said, snatching a coat. "I'm just projecting assuredness." She put the coat on and the sleeves fell about four inches past her hands. "Seriously?"

"You are much shorter than you seem," Martina observed.

"This makes me look like a toddler!"

"Or like you're shrinking. Are you shrinking?" Martina asked Cookie.

"No," Cookie growled, "I'm just short."

"Hey, me, too!" Jay said, flapping his long lab coat sleeves in the air.

"Please stop," Cookie said.

"Maybe roll up the sleeves or something?" Nick asked gingerly.

"Do we have any idea where they might be keeping Ed?" Nick asked as they walked through the warren of hallways underneath Auxano's main building. "Can you hear him at all?" he asked Cookie.

"A little," she said worriedly, "but he's not thinking hard enough about directions."

Farshad put his finger to his lips and pointed to a nearby door marked security. Once past the door Cookie grabbed Martina's arm. "This way," she said, pointing to the door marked stairway. "I think I can hear Ed and you need to tell me if you see him."

Cookie turned to the rest of the group. "Once you've found the blood and the Amish kid, think really hard about how to get to the car. Martina and I will meet you there. If anything goes wrong . . ."

"Run for it." Nick said.

"Exactly," she said, and headed off down a hall with Martina.

"Ah," said Jay, poking his head around the corner. "This is where Nicholas and I must part ways with the rest of you. I believe the blood was taken to a room down this hallway. Are you ready to walk through some walls?" he asked Nick.

"Not really, no," Nick said.

"Excellent!" Jay bowed to Farshad and Abe. "Godspeed," he said seriously, "and we shall see you on the other side."

"Come on," Nick said, grabbing his friend and heading down the hallway. "Good luck," he added quietly over his shoulder.

Farshad looked at Abe. "Let's try to find Willis Fisher," he said.

They quickly discovered two kinds of doors: ones that were unlocked, which led to empty labs, break rooms, and utility closets, and locked ones. Farshad sighed. "He's going to be in a locked room," he said to Abe.

"Ach, yes," Abe said. "How are we going to get in?"

"Well," Farshad said, channeling Jay, "we have super-powers." He reached over to a locked door and pressed his thumb into it. The lock bent like warm butter and the door popped open. Farshad smiled despite himself. Cool.

Inside was someone's office. Farshad shrugged and moved on to the next locked door. Office. Office. Office. Private bathroom. Office. It occurred to Farshad that he was making a huge headache for the Auxano maintenance staff and he felt a little bad about it.

"This is different," Farshad said, stepping into a dark room with what looked like an enormous horizontal window into another room. He took a step closer to look through the window.

"The fire man!" Abe whispered next to him.

Mr. Friend was there, strapped by his wrists and ankles to

a metal bed, just as Farshad had seen him on the video feed in the security office. He was asleep, or possibly drugged. Farshad saw a door to the right of the window that led into Mr. Friend's room.

"What do we do?" Abe asked.

Farshad had no idea. They could rescue Mr. Friend, but how? Could he even wake up? Would they have to carry him out? Plus, what would happen once he was free? Would he go back to setting everything on fire? "I don't know," he admitted.

"Well, we cannot just leave him there, can we?" Abe asked. "He is strapped down."

Farshad leaned his head against the window. Mr. Friend wasn't going anywhere. "Look, if he's here, then your friend is probably somewhere nearby. I say we find Willis and Ed, and then we can come back for Mr. Friend. Then they can help us carry him."

Abe gave him a hard look. "Fine," he said. They left the room, and it seemed to Farshad that their return was pretty unlikely.

NICK WAS TRYING TO LOOK LIKE AN ADULT. THE LAB coat helped—he felt very scientist-y, and at least he wasn't swimming in his coat like Cookie and Jay. He wished he'd had the time to grow a mustache. He couldn't really grow a thick one, but there was definitely hair between his mouth and his nose that he'd taught himself to shave off every few weeks.

After the group had split up, Jay led Nick down a long hallway to the lab where he'd last seen Farshad's vial of blood. Nick stood next to the door, let go of Jay, and a moment later was on the other side. He opened it up.

"Fantastic work, old boy," Jay said, clapping Nick on the back. "Really extraordinary. I feel like you're getting more of a handle on this teleporting business every day."

"Maybe," Nick said. "I still can't go farther than four inches."

"Baby steps, Nicholas, baby steps. Or baby teleports." Jay walked to a large, glass-front refrigeration unit. Inside were rows of vials of what looked like blood. Nick joined him.

"How are we going to be able to tell which one is Farshad's?" Nick asked.

Jay opened the glass door and picked up one of the vials, squinting at the label. "Well this one isn't his," he said, putting it back. "This one belongs to Claire Jones." He put it back and pulled out another vial. Nick leaned in to look at the label.

"Michael Donovan."

"Eric Mathes."

"Emma Lee."

"Siouxsie Rudikoff."

"Izaak Marcus."

Nick looked at Jay. "These are all Company Kids."

Jay wrinkled his brow. "That doesn't make sense. If they were testing Company Kid blood they wouldn't have needed to trick Farshad into giving his with a science field trip cover. Farshad's mother works for Auxano. So does Daniesha's, and her blood isn't here. Ah," he said, "here's Farshad's." Jay wrapped the vial in a sock he had found in his backpack. Hopefully a clean sock.

"So why do they have all this other blood?" Nick wondered, looking at the vials. "They have the blood of every Company Kid I can think of except for Cookie's. Why not Cookie? What's so different about her?"

"She's infinitely more ravishing." Jay grabbed two more vials and put them into his backpack along with Farshad's.

"What are you doing? Put those back!" Nick said. "Don't be a creepy blood thief."

"Hush now," Jay said. "I think we should bring these to our dear Dr. Deery to see if there's anything interesting about them." He put his backpack on. "Mission accomplished. Now stop fretting and let me concentrate on sending beautiful thoughts to Daniesha."

"You're trying to reach her by thinking about Ed's busted old car."

"Anything can be beautiful if you put your mind to it. Let's go."

JAY AND NICK GOT THE BLOOD," COOKIE TOLD MARtina. They had used Dr. Rajavi's access card to descend to the lowest floor of the building with Farshad and Abe, and then split up to look for Ed and Willis Fisher.

"Oh good," Martina said. She looked through the small window of a door. "Empty." They moved on to the next one. "Empty."

Across the hall was a row of hooks with what looked like sound-cancelling headphones hanging off them. Cookie looked at Martina, who shrugged. Cookie stood on the tips of her toes to look into the window of a nearby door. "Huh," she said.

"They look so fluffy," Martina said.

"Wait, didn't Dr. Deery say that he was working with rabbits? What if these are the rabbits?" Cookie asked.

"Should we take one?" Martina asked.

"You want us to steal a bunny?" Cookie asked.

"We'll bring them to Dr. Deery so they can be reunited." Martina tested the doorknob. "Look, it's open," she said, walking into the room. Cookie followed her, and the screaming began.

Cookie had never heard anything so loud in her entire life. It was as if the bunnies were shrieking directly into her brain. The pain in her head was intense, and she clasped her hands to her ears and turned to see Martina doing exactly the same thing. They stumbled out of the room and quickly shut the door behind themselves before dropping to the ground.

Cookie's ears were ringing, and it took a moment for her to realize that there was sound coming out of Martina's moving mouth. "What?" she asked.

"Can you hear me?" Martina asked. Her voice sounded like it was coming through a long, tinny tunnel.

"A little—can you hear me?" Cookie had no idea how loud or soft her voice was. Martina was looking at her and Cookie could see that she was scared. Her eyes flashed different colors; now brown, now gray, now green, now hazel, now a deep blue. Cookie crawled over to Martina and put her hand on the girl's arm and leaned in to put her mouth closer to Martina's ear. "Can you hear me now?" she asked. Martina nodded and seemed to calm down a little. She pointed to the row of sound-cancelling headphones on the wall.

"Well, that answered that question," Cookie said, standing up. She felt wobbly, as if her balance was off. She helped Martina up and the two stumbled down the hall away from the bunny room. "Let's not go back there," Cookie said. Martina nodded.

They had checked out five more rooms before emergency lights in the hallways began to flash. Martina and

Cookie looked at each other. "Did you touch anything?" Cookie asked. Martina shook her head and looked expectantly at Cookie. "I didn't touch anything!" Cookie said. She could hardly hear her own voice.

Farshad and Abe were almost upon them before Cookie and Martina noticed them. They were running and half dragging a pale teenage boy in a hospital gown.

"RUN!" Farshad yelled at Cookie and Martina.

"What? Where? Why?"

"I used my thumbs to break down the door to his room and set off some sort of alarm! We have to get out of here!" Far down the hall Cookie could see two security guards running toward them. She turned and ran until Martina stopped at the row of headphones.

Martina grabbed Abe and put a pair of headphones over his ears. Cookie caught a pair that Martina threw at her. "WHAT ARE YOU DOING?" she asked, putting the headphones on as Martina tossed two more pairs to Farshad and the boy in the hospital gown. "WE HAVE TO RUN!"

"WE'RE GOING IN THE WRONG DIRECTION!" Martina yelled, and dragged Abe into the screaming bunny room. She emerged with a bunny in each hand and handed one to Cookie. She pointed the other one at the oncoming security guards.

Cookie watched as Martina's bunny opened its mouth and the security guards careened to a stop and clutched

their heads in pain. Cookie pointed her own bunny in the same direction and the agonized guards fell to the ground. Cookie turned to Martina, who pointed to the hallway beyond the twitching guards. Abe grabbed the Amish kid and threw him over his shoulder and they all ran, jumping over the bodies of the guards.

The sound-cancelling headphones were incredibly effective—Cookie couldn't hear a thing as they ran through the hallways, and yet there was Jay's voice in her head, shouting directions. *TURN LEFT HERE! THE DOOR AT THE END OF THE HALL TO YOUR RIGHT!* Cookie hurled herself at the door that opened up to a large parking lot and held it open as a beet-faced Abe carried the boy through. Farshad and Martina were close behind—

HELP!

Cookie turned around to see that another two guards had grabbed Jay. She panicked and hurled her bunny at them. The guards dropped Jay and fell to the ground while the bunny hopped around them and sniffed their twitching feet. Cookie grabbed Jay and yanked him out the door, where Farshad was waiting. Once they were out, he pressed his thumbs into the doorknob, squishing it like a marshmallow, and then did the same to the hinges before beckoning Jay and Cookie to run.

They tore off their glaringly white lab coats and threw them to the ground, and as they skittered through the dark parking lot Jay was babbling and Cookie was extra grateful for the headphones. They crashed through the tree line into the woods, where they were finally hidden from the lights of the Auxano parking lot. Now she couldn't hear and she could hardly see. Cookie gingerly took off her headphones. Farshad did the same.

"What was that?" Jay yelled excitedly. Nick clasped his hand over Jay's mouth.

Cookie was beginning to hear better but there was still an annoying whine in her head. Jay kept talking through Nick's hand. "That *hurt*! Were those *sonic* rabbits? Did we just take out four armed security guards with *bunnies*???"

Cookie's eyes widened. "Were those security guards *armed*?"

Farshad put his finger up to his lips. "You're being really loud," he said. Cookie wrinkled her nose at him. "We can talk about all of this when we're safe." He turned to Jay. "Did you get the blood?"

"What?" Jay asked, and Nick nodded.

Cookie took out her phone and used it as a flashlight to find the path through the woods that they'd used to get from Ed's car to Auxano. As they reached the road Cookie could see the others, and was horrified to realize that Martina was still holding on to her rabbit.

"Your ears!" Cookie yelped. "Cover your ears!" She

fumbled to put the headphones back on before noticing that Martina and the others had taken theirs off. Martina gestured for her to take them off.

"It's okay," she said, "Abe asked Howler to please be quiet, and she seemed amenable to his request."

Cookie stared at the bunny, who wrinkled its nose at her. Jay took a step toward the bunny. Cookie grabbed a handful of his sweater to stop him. "Do. Not. Annoy. That. Bunny," she growled. "We should probably get out of here. Fast."

"What are we going to do with him?" Nick asked, looking at the Amish kid who was slumped against Ed's car. "And did we get Ed? Is he here?"

"We didn't see him," Cookie said.

"Well, technically, no one can see him," Jay pointed out. "So he might be with us RIGHT NOW."

"No, he's not," Martina said. "We weren't able to find him before the security alarms went off."

"We can't just leave him in there." Nick said.

"We can't go back," Cookie said. "Even if they weren't looking for us there's an insane screaming bunny roaming the halls."

"Then what are we supposed to do with his car? We can't just leave it on the side of the road." Nick said, and they all turned to look at Abe.

"Sis en ayland," Abe breathed, clearly terrified.

Farshad opened the passenger side door and helped Willis Fisher into the car, gently buckling him in. "You can do this, man," he said to Abe, awkwardly patting him on the back.

Martina climbed into the back of the car and buckled herself in. Cookie stared. "Wait, where are you going?"

Martina held up the rabbit. "Howler has to stay with Abe or else he might start screaming again."

A car passed them on the darkened road, and Cookie became very aware of how exposed they all were. She got into the car. "We all need to go," she said. "Turn on the headlights," she told Abe.

"Smart. So smart!" Jay exclaimed, diving into the car and squishing up next to her. "This is nice," he said.

"I am very not dealing with you right now."

"Well, I'm the smallest anyway, so I'll jump in the back." Jay scrambled over the backseat into the hatchback trunk of Ed's car. Farshad got in the car with a grim look on his face.

"This is insane. There's no room!" Nick said, throwing his hands up in the air.

"Get in the car, old man!" Jay said.

"No. NO. This is not happening. I just broke into a highly secure corporate facility, aided and abetted in the stealing of blood, a rabbit, and an entire other human being, and now you want me to get into a car with five other people and a driver who has NEVER DRIVEN A CAR BEFORE. Does anyone else see how crazy—"

"STOP!" A white van that looked exactly like the one that had absconded with Mr. Friend a few days before had come to a screeching halt in front of them while Nick had been ranting. Four men in hazmat suits came out.

"YOU DON'T KNOW WHAT YOU'RE DOING," the lead hazmat said. "JUST COME WITH US AND EVERYTHING—"

"TAKE HOWLER!!!" Cookie screamed, grabbing Howler from Martina and holding her out to Nick. She clasped her hands over Nick's ears as he took Howler from her and pointed the small, fluffy bunny at the men from the van.

"DON'T MAKE ME USE THIS!" Cookie heard Nick shout before hastily putting on her own headphones and returning her hands to his ears. She watched in horrified fascination as the men dropped to the ground, writhing in agony. Cookie scrambled to sit on Martina's lap as Nick backed into the car.

GO GO GO! She saw Nick's mouth form the words as he closed the door. Abe turned the key in the ignition and put his shaky hands on the gearshift. The entire car shuddered.

Cookie looked over to Howler, whose mouth was now closed. She took off her headphones and reached into the front seat to take off Abe's. "PUT YOUR FOOT ON THE BRAKE BEFORE YOU SHIFT GEARS!" she yelled.

He complied and put the car in Drive. "Now what???"

Cookie could see the men from Auxano in the rearview mirror stumbling to get up.

"TAKE YOUR FOOT OFF THE BRAKE, PUT IT ON THE GAS PEDAL AND GET US OUT OF HERE!" she screamed.

Abe jammed his foot down and the car lurched forward, knocking Cookie backward. Martina grabbed her around the waist like a human safety belt as Cookie tried not to scream in fear.

"TURN! TURN AROUND!" Farshad yelled, his sound-cancelling headphones still on. "WE'RE HEADED STRAIGHT BACK TO AUXANO!"

Abe wrenched the steering wheel to the right and the car's tires squealed angrily on the pavement as Ed's car spun out of control. "BRAKE!!! BRAKE!!! OTHER PEDAL!" Cookie and Farshad yelled in unison, and the car came to a halt directly facing the Auxano van. The men in hazmat suits began running toward the car.

"GUN IT!" Farshad yelled.

"I DO NOT HAVE A GUN!" Abe screamed.

"GAS PEDAL! GAS PEDAL! THE ONE ON THE RIGHT! GO!!!" Cookie shrieked, and once again the car shot forward.

"WHEEEEEEE!!!" Jay screamed from the back of the car.

The Auxano men saw Ed's car barreling toward them and threw themselves to the side of the road. "THE VAN!"

Nick yelled, and Abe swerved to get out of the way but still scraped the entire side of the van and knocked off its side-view mirror. The sound of metal against metal was too much for Howler to handle and the poor bunny started scream-ing again. Martina instinctively clapped her hands over her ears, sending Cookie flying across Farshad's and Nick's laps. She grabbed the bunny from Nick. "SHUT UP, BUNNY!" she yelled. The bunny stopped.

"Did I do that?" she asked, astonished.

"No, I did," Abe said. He was pale as a sheet but driving in a relatively straight line down the road.

"Good job," Martina said. "Where are we going?"

"Lancaster." Abe said. "We have to bring Willis to my sister."

They all looked at the boy in the hospital gown who was giggling quietly to himself. "'S macht nix aus," he said softly. "'S macht nix aus."

Cookie crawled back over Farshad and Nick to get back on Martina's lap. "This just keeps getting better and better."

Howler nuzzled her chin as they drove through the night.

NICK FOUGHT TO KEEP FROM THROWING UP. HE'D never had the stomach for bad driving, and Abe clearly didn't really know how to drive; Cookie and Farshad had to talk him through every step.

"That stick on the side of the steering wheel. Pull it down before you turn left."

"And up before you turn right."

"No, that's the windshield wiper. The stick on the other side of the steering wheel."

"Stop that. You can put your foot on the gas or the brake, but not both."

Nick tried not to think too hard about the fact that the two people advising the unlicensed driver had also never driven a car, and they lurched through the back country roads until they got to the outskirts of Lancaster. Cookie used the map function on her phone to direct Abe to Rebecca's, and with a deep sigh of relief he pulled Ed's car into the driveway of his sister's house and put it in park.

"That was magnificent!" Jay said, bounding out of the back. "Although I can't say I'm pleased with the amount of sculpture tools that Ed seems to keep back here. They're sharp. I'm injured. No matter! Good work, you glorious chauffeur." He grabbed Abe's hand and shook it vigorously as Abe slumped against the side of the car with a glazed look in his eyes. "And you were an exquisite navigator," Jay added to Cookie, who rolled her eyes.

Nick smiled a little despite himself, and then went with Farshad to help Willis Fisher out of the car. The Amish teen was still muttering to himself in Pennsylvania Dutch and seemed incapable of walking without aid.

"Do you think they drugged him?" Nick asked Farshad as they walked up to the house.

"I don't know what they did to him," Farshad said, holding Willis awkwardly to avoid using his thumbs.

"I wonder what they're doing to Mr. Friend," Nick wondered. Farshad said nothing.

"Willis!" Rebecca exclaimed as they entered the apartment. She clutched her hands together fearfully and began speaking in Pennsylvania Dutch with Abe, who seemed to be telling her the story of how they'd rescued Willis (and why her apartment was suddenly filled with strange people). A hulking teenage boy rushed up to them and gently led Willis to the ugly plaid sofa. Nick awkwardly stood nearby.

Abe had finished his story and Rebecca surveyed the group. "My brother and Willis can stay here but the rest of you have to get back home."

"Uh, how, exactly?" Farshad asked.

Rebecca looked at the big guy who was putting a blanket

over Willis. "Beanie can bring you back to Muellersville in the invisible man's car," she said, "he knows how to drive. And then we have to hide the car," she said, mostly to herself.

"But wait, wait," Jay said, "we need answers, and your incoherent friend has them. Can we just talk to him before we go?" Jay knelt by Willis, who was looking agitated, and began to speak in rapid-fire Pennsylvania Dutch while pointing at Martina.

"I am sorry," Beanie said, perplexed, "he wants your book."

Martina clutched her sketchbook to her chest. "No," she whispered. "He can't have it."

"Not a problem, not a problem at all," Jay said, opening up his backpack and pulling out a lined notebook and a pen. Willis snatched them and sat up on the couch, scribbling furiously. Everyone slowly crept closer to see what he was writing.

Nick looked at Farshad. "I've got no idea," Farshad said.

"Fascinating," Jay said.

"Is he, like, completely nuts now?" Cookie asked. "I mean, was he always like this or did Auxano make him this freaky?"

Rebecca looked like she was about to cry. "Willis?" she

asked softly, putting her hand on his shoulder. He kept writing as if he hadn't heard her. "Willis, vass is sell?" A tear rolled down her cheek. "What did they do to you?"

What did they do to all of us? Nick wondered, watching as Willis continued to scribble and mutter. He looked up and saw that Cookie was looking at him. Had she read his mind?

Probably not. She was most likely just thinking the exact same thing.

BEANIE WAS A MUCH BETTER DRIVER THAN ABE, although when Cookie thought about it, that really wasn't saying much. When she began to wonder how an Amish teenager in hiding from Auxano got a driver's license in the first place, she decided that it was probably best not to think about it at all.

Truth be told, there was a whole lot she'd rather not be thinking about.

Beanie pulled up to Nick's aunts' house first and parked the car.

"Thank you so much, good sir," Jay told him, "you are a gentleman and an excellent friend, and I do hope we will see each other again under more pleasant circumstances." He leaned over Nick to open the passenger side door.

"Wait," said Beanie. He'd hardly spoken a word the whole trip except to take directions from Cookie and Farshad. He turned around to look at them.

"We should never have gone with that woman and given her our blood and done those tests," Beanie continued. "That was our first mistake."

"You couldn't have known what she was going to do to you," Farshad said.

"I knew that it was a lot of money for doing very little. Good people don't give you money for nothing. You're going to have to pay, sooner or later, and I knew that. We were greedy, and now we've been shunned, Sadie and Jesse are gone, and Willis . . ."

"Maybe he'll be all right after a while," Nick said. Beanie gave him a hard look, and even though it was dark in the car, Cookie could see Nick's cheeks turning red.

"Our second mistake is that we told people about what we could do," Beanie said. "We told our families, they didn't understand, and then we lost everything. Everything. I was going to work with my father in his saddle shop. I was going to be a saddler, like him. Now that will never happen. Never." Beanie's voice trembled and he took a deep breath. "I never thought our own families would turn on us, but they did. You can't trust anyone except each other, because no one else will understand.

"Our third mistake was that we split up. We left Willis behind, and now we have no idea where Sadie and Jesse are. We don't know what their powers have done to them. For all we know, they could be like Willis. Rebecca and I might be next." Beanie was gripping the steering wheel, and Cookie could see that his knuckles had turned white. She looked at Martina, whose eyes also flickered to Beanie's hands.

"Sadie and Jesse left because they were scared to stay. We stayed because we were scared to leave. I still don't know who made the right choice, but I know that we should have stayed together." Beanie turned his head to slowly look at all of them. "You are in this together," he said, his voice now firm. "Don't make the same mistakes we made. Whatever happens, no one is going to know you like the other people in this car. And possibly the strange little guy," he said, looking warily at Jay, who for once was not smiling like a great big goober. "Do you understand?"

Everyone in the car was silent. "Yes," said Cookie after a moment.

"Yes," said Martina.

"Yes, we understand," said Nick.

"Okay," said Farshad.

"Absolutely," said Jay.

WELL, LOOK AT THIS!" FARSHAD'S MOTHER burst into his room with a copy of *The Muellersville Sun*. He rubbed his eyes and groaned. People needed to start knocking. Or to start assuming that if he was in his room with his door closed that he didn't want to be bothered.

"What?" he said. "What are we looking at?"

"It doesn't say your name, but I'm pretty sure it's about you!" his mother said excitedly, shoving the paper under his nose. Farshad, suddenly very awake, grabbed the paper, looking furiously for news of last night's break-in at Auxano headquarters. His mother pointed to an article and read over his shoulder.

* * *

The Muelle

Record-breaking Test Scores Propel Muellersville to Best in State

An astonishing 32 percent of Deborah Read Middle School students have found themselves with Academic Honors after an incredibly impressive showing at the National Achievement Exams this past weekend. "It's incredible," gushed Maureen Jacobs, the school's principal, "but not surprising. The students and faculty at Deborah Read have been working so hard, and this is the natural result."

With so many perfect or near-perfect test scores, there was an initial suspicion of cheating or tampering, but state officials have examined all of the materials and declared the exam results to be "100 percent aboveboard."

"I've never seen anything like it," said Professor Dogan, the chair of the education department at nearby Lancaster University. "It's an incredible jump up from last year's test scores, but everything is squeaky clean. These are just really, really smart kids."

The high percentage of excellent scores makes Deborah Read the highest achieving middle school in Pennsylvania. "People think we're just a little hick town in the middle of nowhere," Muellersville Mayor Rick Wilkins said. "But we've got a thriving, walkable downtown, a great neighbor and corporate partner in Auxano, and now the smartest kids in the state! It's paradise!"

Farshad scanned the rest of the paper before putting it down, his heart rate returning to normal as he saw no signs of the previous night's madness. Dr. Rajavi was looking for his reaction to the article. "Wow," he said.

"Now I know that having everyone do well might hurt your chances of being valedictorian, but don't worry, I'm sure you're still doing much better on the regular exams," Dr. Rajavi said, choosing to ignore his nonchalance. She was clearly thrilled. "Maybe next time they'll put your actual name in the paper! I'm sure they'll have all of the high scorers up on the main bulletin board at school; I wish the paper had waited until seeing that before they printed the story. Ah well. Get dressed and come have some breakfast." She gave Farshad a kiss on the top of his head and skipped out of the room.

Farshad frowned. He was fairly confident that he'd done well on the exam, but had 32 percent of his classmates done as well? Sure, he expected high scores from the other smart kids like Kitty Faber and Emma Lee, and there were always those weird kids who performed well on exams, like Jay, but 32 percent? It made no sense. Farshad had a sinking feeling.

About an hour later he stood in front of the school's main bulletin board, looking up at the names of the kids with the highest scores. The school secretary had written out all of the names on colorful construction paper and decorated each one with shiny star stickers.

HIGH ACHIEVERS
Claire Jones
Farshad Rajavi
Eric Mathes
Michael Donovan
Emma Lee
Izaak Marcus
Souxie Rudikoff
Jay Carpenter

THE DAILY WHUT?

Something is rotten in the state of Auxano. No one is talking about it (SURPRISE, SURPRISE) but I have it on good authority that there was a break in at the Auxano main campus LAST NIGHT. Sure, the authorities there are telling the public that it was "a security system malfunction that has since been fixed" but does that explain the several security guards that were taken to Muellersville Hospital under the cover of darkness? Or the discarded lab coats that my sources say were found at the edge of the forest that surrounds the campus?

There's only one explanation, friends: Violent streaking nudists have stolen something from Auxano, something that our benevolent corporate benefactors would rather we didn't know about. Now it is well known that most streakers are gentle people who just want to be free of clothing, but whoever broke into the labs was On. A. Mission. We can't be certain of what they took, but whatever it was, it's got the administrators at Auxano sweating bullets.

THE DAILY WHUT?

Now I know I've been quick to suspect our overlords at Auxano of wrongdoing in the past, but something real is happening and I, your intrepid Hammer, will be the one to find out exactly what it is. Until then, friends, when you see a naked person you'd best run in the other direction.

Always beware,

The Hammer

OOKIE AND MARTINA DIDN'T TALK MUCH DURING the long bus trip to Philadelphia. Cookie had told her mom that she was spending the day with Addison and Claire. It was a lie, and Cookie was not happy with the way those were stacking up. But she'd made up her mind to accompany Martina to Philadelphia, in no small part because Addison and Claire hadn't actually bothered to invite her over. Spending the day with Martina wasn't really high on her list of fun things to do, but it was better than doing nothing.

Dr. Deery was surprised to see them. "Hey," he said, looking around as he ushered them into the building, "Ed, where are you?"

"He's not with us," Cookie explained, as Martina took the stolen vials of blood out of her backpack to give to Dr. Deery. "There were some problems at Auxano."

Dr. Deery paled. "What sort of problems?"

Behind Cookie a cell phone buzzed on the counter of the old butcher shop. She caught a quick look at the screen before Dr. Deery picked up the phone and pocketed it. "My girlfriend," he explained, "I'll call her back later. What sort of problems?"

ACKNOWLEDGMENTS

Thank you, once again, to all the incredible people at Abrams Books who just won't stop being awesome all the time: Jason Wells, Chad Beckerman, Caitlin Miller, Pam Notarantonio, and of course, the ever-magical Susan Van Metre.

Many thanks to Tori Doherty-Munro at Writers House and to my agent and guiding light Dan Lazar, who is really very patient with me when I've had a little caffeine and can't stop telling him all of my ideas at once.

I want to send deep gratitude to all the readers who have sent me the most wonderful notes throughout the years—I deeply wish I had the time to answer each one. But I don't! Because I have so many stories I still want to tell you.

No thanks whatsoever go to my cat, Dr. Josephine Frimplepants. You are too loud at 3:30 AM. Get it together.

And last of all thanks to my friends and family, in particular Mark, Anya, and Ezra, for all the hugs. I get so many hugs, you guys. Everyone should get so many hugs.

AMY IGNATOW

is the author and illustrator of the Popularity Papers series and *The Mighty Odds*. She lives in Philadelphia with her family and doesn't get enough sleep. Her cat is loud.